as waters gone by

Tina Bustamante

As Waters Gone By

Contact Information: leapbks@gmail.com

Cover Art by Leap Books

Leap Books
Powell, WY
www.leapbks.net

Publishing History
First Leap Edition 2013
ISBN: 978-1-61603-029-2

Library of Congress Control Number: 2013950450

Published in the United States of America

dedication

For my husband, Rodrigo,
and for
David and Daniel.

In memory of
Violeta de La Luz Gallegos
1949-1986

acknowledgments

I want to thank my dear family who tirelessly asked me about this book: My mom, Rachael, Judi, Katie, Karissa, and my dad. For David, Daniel, Rianne and Sherah. Thank you all for your endless encouragement. Thank you to Leslie Gould who edited and gave suggestions in the early stages of this project. For Heather Clayton, Judi Ballantyne, Sally McCleery, and Christy Freriks who made kind suggestions and were willing readers. For Rodrigo, Emma, and Lucas, thank you for loving me and believing. For Patrick Carman who suggested I write another book. For my editor, Kat O'Shea, who put in nearly as many hours as I did and pushed me, believing in this story. From the bottom of my heart, I thank you.

"You will forget your sorrow, recalling it only as waters gone by."

~ Zophar the Naamathite

one day before

I sit in the back seat, my left hand gripping my backpack. I fidget and I bite my fingernails and stare out the window, counting the minutes till we're home. I hate bumming rides. After today, I won't have to ever again.

A gentle mist covers the street in the wet gloss of early spring. The air is moist with new life blooming. Fresh flowers are everywhere, in hanging baskets, in pots, in the ground. Winter is finally over, and the ground is warming up.

Maria and I are riding home from school with Michael. She's had a crush on him the last two years of high school, and I think something's finally going to happen between them. I'm happy for her, but their flirting is driving me crazy. I keep checking the time on my phone.

Michael's Hybrid Civic pulls into my trailer park. He stops his car between our two trailers, and I pick up my backpack to get out. He's one of the few we trust to come inside our trailer park. Most of the kids at school know we live here. Very few have ever been invited to actually see which trailer is mine. Michael's different. I push my way out of the backseat as fast as I can. Maria lets me through, but lingers with Michael.

Her older brother, Jose, steps outside when I get out of the car. We've grown up together, and he's pretty much my best friend. His hair is cut short, his jeans are dirty, his feet are bare. He's strong and muscular from hours of hard work. He leans against the rickety metal railing. I'm half expecting it to collapse under him as it moans in protest. The trailer is so old we all wonder how it manages to stay upright.

He gives me a quick nod as I climb the stairs to my front door. "When do you want to head out, Ellie?" His eyes light up with excitement and pride. He knows this is one of the most important days of my life.

I beam at him. "I want to count everything one more time. I'll be ready in about twenty minutes."

"You want me to come over?"

I shake my head. "No, I'll be quick.

He turns to go back inside. "Just text me when you're ready. I'm going to take a shower."

I crinkle my nose and make a brisk waving motion with my hand. "Good idea."

After unlocking my door, I step inside, and the room reeks of the sweet lingering smell of pot. At least there are no used needles around. Marijuana's bad enough, but the other stuff is terrible.

Mom's a bartender down the road. She'll be home in an hour for her break and then won't be back till about midnight or so. I have to get out of here with my money before she sees it. I push my way through the stale smoke to my bedroom.

The envelope of cash is hidden inside my jewelry box, and the box is tucked in the back of my sock drawer. Thousands of hours of babysitting. Three thousand dollars. Four years of saving. I've taken care of more runny-nosed little kids than I should ever admit to. Kids are great, but honestly, I'm another mother to some of them. It's all been worth it though, because today Jose is taking me to pick up my brand-new car. Brand-new to me, at least.

A Subaru Outback with like a million miles on it, but the guy from the dealership says these cars were made to go two million, and he's giving me a deal. I have just enough money. It doesn't hurt that his eight-year-old son, Jorge, tells him all the time how wonderful I am.

I'm running the bills through my fingers, breathing in the green smell of freedom, counting each one again, just to make sure all three thousand dollars are still there when a motorcycle roars up to the trailer. My hands freeze, my mind stops counting. Oh no. I don't have time to deal with any of my mom's crap right now. I have to get to the dealership. Nothing's going to mess this up. I'm shoving my money back into its hiding place when footsteps clomp up the metal stairs.

Someone bangs on the door. "Rose, open the door. Where's my money?"

Oh God. I hide behind my door. The heat of my heavy breathing warms my face. I silently curse my mother.

He hits the door harder. "Rose! I swear to God I'll find you and kill you. You owe me too much. I'm not going away."

It's her boyfriend—aka drug dealer—Jazz. Who dates a guy named Jazz? It has drug dealer written all over it.

My mother is someone who dates guys named Jazz.

My hands tremble. My breathing is so loud, the neighbors can probably hear me. I have to do something. I take a deep breath. I have to get her out of this mess. Most of her past boyfriends were all smoke and bluff. Not Jazz.

I tiptoe to the door, trying to get my breathing under control, but open it real quick when he starts another pounding-on-the-door episode. "Rose is gone," I say with as much bravado as I can muster. "What can I do for you?"

He steps back, and I take it all in – black boots, dark

jeans, a leather jacket, leather gloves with the tops ripped off so his fingers protrude, a spiked metal collar, and pitch-black eyes that glare at me with a hatred that stops my breath.

"Where's Rose?" He edges closer to me. I gag on the smell of grease and stale cigarettes.

"She's gone. What's going on, Jazz?" I say his name real decidedly, trying to give off a don't-mess-with-me vibe, but he's not the sort to be intimidated by a teenage girl.

He gets in my face. "Where is she, Ellie?" He mimics the exact same tone I used.

How does he know my name? My mom talks about him all the time. But she doesn't like guys to know she's old enough to have a teenage daughter, so I stay incognito. "She's not here. What's the problem?"

His smile turns his eyes even darker. "I need to find her. Your mother is not going to weasel her way out of this one. No matter how cute you are."

I clench my fists and struggle to unclench them. I stare at him and then glance past him, hoping Jose is standing on his porch. He's not. I'm alone.

Jazz looks me up and down with his dark eyes. "You're a hot little thing, aren't you? I might be willing to lower the debt if you invited me in for a few minutes."

I hate my mother. I stare at the wall and bite my lip. "How much does she owe?" My voice is quiet. Furious.

"Five thousand. And I swear to God, if she doesn't give me the money today, I'll kill her. Her sweet talk ain't gonna work this time." He places his arm against the door. "Like I said, I'm willing to work out a deal with you, though." His cold black eyes rake me from head to toe like I'm a meal he's dying to savor. Gross.

My stomach lurches. I take a breath. He scratches his head and winks, waiting for my response. His wiry body is strong, and as he flashes me a snake-charmer of a smile, I realize he will kill her. He's not kidding. It's not like I have a whole lot of options. Disgust sinks into my gut. "Hold on a minute."

I hurry back to my room and yank open the sock drawer. I grab my money and slam the drawer. I take one last look at my dream. My shoulders slump. The hard-earned money that I hid so carefully from my mom. I was so scared she'd steal it for drugs.

It wasn't supposed to be like this. Something good was finally going to happen to me.

I give Jazz the fiercest look I have in me, take two steps toward him, and thrust out the envelope. "Here. It's not the full five thousand, but it's more than you'll ever get from my mom."

His eyebrows shoot up. He opens the envelope and rifles through the money. "This yours?"

"It doesn't matter whose it is. Take it. It's clean. I didn't sell drugs to get it."

He leers at me with a sick grin on his face.

"I didn't do what you're thinking either."

He laughs and slaps the envelope on the palm of his hand, making a clapping sound. "I'm sure you didn't. We can't all be as good as you." He cups my cheek and runs his thumb across it.

I stagger backwards. He sneers as the envelope disappears into his coat pocket. I put my hand over my mouth, trying hard not to vomit. Every penny is gone. Along with all my dreams. My future car is in some scum's pocket.

"Make sure you tell Rose I was here," he says.

I grab the door to close it in his face. He turns and takes the steps in two strides, hops on his motorcycle, and rides off. The vibrations of his chopper ride up my arm uninvited, making me shiver.

I'm shell-shocked. Alone. Tired. Broke. Defeated. And much more that I can't put into words. I sink onto the couch, trying to remember how to inhale and exhale, trying to hold it all together. The cloud of hopelessness descends so fast, I can't see straight.

Jose knocks on the door. "Ellie?"

I don't respond.

The door squeaks open. He takes one look at me and frowns. "What's going on? You ready to pick up your car?"

I stare at the brown-stained carpet, run my hand across my forehead, force myself to look at him. "It's gone."

"What's gone?"

"The money. All of it." I give him a mock smile. "Guess there'll be no car for me."

Jose takes two steps into the house. His eyes flash. "Your mom got it? I told you like a hundred times to find a good hiding place. You should of left it at my house."

I put my head in my hands. "It's not like that. Jazz came."

Jose presses his back against the wall. The flimsy wall sways back and forth trying to decide whether or not it will hold him up. "What happened?"

"He threatened to kill her. Said she owes him five thousand. What could I do?"

Jose waves his arms in the air. "Let your mom figure it out. If she was worried he'd kill her, she could have gone to the police or something."

"Yeah, like she's going to admit to the police that she owes her boyfriend drug money. We're not talking pot here, Jose. He would have killed her. You don't mess around with Jazz. Remember Silly Sally?"

Jose crosses his arms and gives a quick nod.

Sally was one of my mom's druggie friends who owed Jazz money. The police are still trying to find her.

Jose paces, his lips pinched together. He squeezes his hands into fists, releases them, and then squeezes again. He turns to the wall and punches it. The house trembles with the reverberations.

I jump up and grab his arm. "Jose, it's fine."

"No, it's not. It not fine at all, Ellie. Why didn't you

come over? I would have helped you figure it out."

I tighten my grip and force him to look at me. "He was here. He was threatening to kill her. Among other things. I didn't have a choice."

Jose's eyes turn dark. He takes my face in his hands. "Did he hurt you? He didn't do anything to you, did he?"

I look down, avoiding his gaze. "I value the price of my virginity more than the Subaru." My eyes well with tears.

"Ellie." He pulls me into his arms. "This is so messed up."

I bury my face in his shirt and breathe in fresh-cut lawn and Ivory Soap®. He has one arm around me and one hand on my head, stroking my hair.

We stay there for a minute. I let him hold me, trying to pretend it's going to be all right. He rests his chin against my head. "What time is she coming home?"

"Soon. For her break. She's working the late shift."

"Want to come over?"

I keep my head against his chest for another moment. My voice sounds muffled. "Not yet. I'm going to wait for her."

He kisses the top of my head. "Just come over after that, OK? I don't want you to sit here by yourself all night."

"'K."

I wait in the silence of my trailer. My mind races faster and faster. I saved for years. I scrimped. I didn't buy lattes. I didn't go to the movies with friends. I shopped at budget and consignment stores. While she spends money she doesn't even have on drugs.

My stomach is hollow.

My mind is numb.

My heart is shattered.

And then, out of the ashes of my crushed dreams rises

a ferocious rage with its own life force, exploding out of me. I'm done being nice to my mom. I'm sick and tired of letting her get away with everything. I'm finished with it.

She stumbles in a few minutes later. I'm slumped on the couch with my arms crossed – a meager attempt to hold in my pain. My hair is drooping over my shoulders. Her blonde hair is in a perky ponytail.

She sees me and jumps back. "Ellie, what are you doing sitting there? You scared me to death."

"Waiting for you."

She scours the room, glancing everywhere, but seeing nothing. "Don't you have anyone to babysit?" Her voice is tight, and she's opening and closing her fists. She lifts a slat and peeks through the blinds with shaking hands. "I'm in a real tight spot," she says, shutting the blinds. They rattle. "Jazz is looking all over the city for me. They covered for me at the bar, but I don't know how long I can keep him off my trail. We need to move."

I sigh. "We don't need to move. Jazz isn't looking for you anymore."

She startles. "What does that mean?"

"He was already here."

She stops fidgeting and finally her eyes lock onto mine. "You didn't let him in, did you?"

"He pounded on the door so hard I thought it was going to fall off."

She pushes the wisps of hair off her face with both hands and sits on the small table next to the front door. Even though she's only thirty-six, all the wrinkles on her face make her look fifty. Her eyes are sunken, and she never meets people's eyes. "What did you tell him?" Her words are more like gasps. "You covered for me, right?"

That sends me over the edge. I. Am. Sixteen. I'm supposed to be the kid here. My mom is asking if I lied to her heroin dealer. "Are you crazy?" I fling out my arms. "He's your drug dealer. How exactly am I supposed to cover for you?"

She slumps in the chair and buries her face in her hands. "Tell him I left town, tell him you don't know where I am. Anything. Ellie, Jazz is no one to mess with."

I stiffen, clenching my teeth and glaring at her. "I took care of it. Like always.

Her head jerks up. "What did you do?"

"What do you think, I did? Pay him off with sex?"

"That's not even funny." Her voice is breathy. Guilty. Her eyes remain fixed on the dark brown carpet, stained with years of life.

"Who's laughing?" I stare at her so hard it forces her to look at me. "I gave him all my money is what I did."

She exhales in relief. "I'll pay you back. I promise."

That is such crap. "How in the world are you going to pay me back? You can't even cover the rent."

"I'm trying, Ellie."

"No you're not. You quit trying years ago, and we both know it."

"I'll pay you back. At least we won't have Jazz breathing down our necks. You did the right thing."

He wouldn't have been breathing down my neck if she hadn't gotten herself into the mess in the first place. She's out of her mind. "The right thing?" I yell. "I paid off your drug dealer!" I slam my hand against the coffee table. "We live in a trailer park. You're a freaking mess and always have been."

"I'm sorry, Ellie."

"I gave him three thousand dollars. You'll never come up with that money. It'll just be some other drug dealer, some other debt. I'm sick and tired of picking up the pieces of your life. I'm done covering for you."

She hunches over and stares at the floor again. "I'll try to do better."

"Whatever, Mom. We both know that's not going to happen. I hate you."

What comes next are words that I'll always regret, words I'll never get back.

as waters gone by

I jerk open the door, and it bangs against the trailer's frame as I run to Jose's house.

two hours before

I wake to the sound of hot oil sizzling in Guadalupe's frying pan. She cracks the eggs, and they hit the pan so loudly, they dance down the hall to the room where I'm sleeping. Spicy scrambled eggs are my favorite. It takes a minute to remember why I'm in their trailer. Then I cringe, shoving my face into my pillow. God, I want to disappear.

A few minutes later, I stumble down the narrow hallway, the orange shag carpet tickling my bare feet. My dark hair hangs loose down my back; and the curls are tighter than normal from the Seattle humidity.

Jose is standing in the kitchen, shirtless, drinking chocolate milk from the carton. *"Buenos dias."* He holds the carton out, offering me a swig.

"Morning," I mutter. I raise my eyebrows. "Could you pass me a glass?"

He laughs softly. "Is drinking out of the carton beneath you?"

"Oh please," I say as he hands me a cup.

He fills it for me and then kisses my cheek. "You OK?" He gives me his trademark stare that pushes past the outer layers of my normal put-togetherness and demands to know the truth.

"I'll manage." I step over to Guadalupe, and she sticks out her cheek for the same greeting.

Jose and I sit down at the table as Guadalupe sets the tortillas next to me and puts the spicy eggs in the middle of the table. Jose dishes up a spoonful. Guadalupe places her hands on my shoulders. "What you gonna do, *hija*?"

Her soft words constrict my throat.

I shake my head and can't believe what I'm about to say. "Go home and do what I always do. Make sure she's all right and clean up the mess."

Jose doesn't respond, and by the way he grips his fork, his knuckles turning white and all, he's so furious he can't talk. They've watched me fix things for my mom for years, and he's sick of it.

He doesn't finish his breakfast. He stands, lips pinched together, and shoves his plate into the sink. I flinch. He walks over to me and moves my hair to the side. He squeezes my shoulder for a moment. He's probably trying to figure out what to do, what to say, but there's nothing to say. Nothing to make this better.

After a minute, he goes to the shower. I close my eyes, trying to keep the tears from escaping. I don't want to cry. I want to stay mad. I don't want to give my mom – or that damn Jazz – the satisfaction of seeing how heartbroken I am. Without thinking, I twist my rings, winding them around and around my cold fingers. I count them. Seven silver rings.

I take another bite, stand, and glance at Guadalupe. "*Gracias por la comida.*"

She walks me to the door and takes my hand before I step into the brisk, spring air. She says in Spanish, "She's your only mother, Ellie." Then she pushes the hair out of my face and stares hard into all the secrets places inside of me.

I close my eyes and lower my head, biting my lip. "I know. That's why I'm going home." I fake a smile.

After she closes the door behind me, I stand on the porch, take a deep breath, and text Maria, telling her that I'll come by later to get a free coffee and to steal her tip money, because I'm poor again. I walk down their porch steps, into the narrow alley, to my trailer.

one hour later

That's when I find her.

I call 911. They rush over, take us to the hospital, wheel her to the back, and tell me to get out of the way. Nurses whip by me, people shout code this, code that. I stand in the entryway until someone guides me to the waiting room.

Guadalupe, Maria, and Jose meet me at the hospital. Jose is the only one who thinks clearly enough to ask for my aunt's name. The only aunt I know is my mom's older sister, who lives on Orcas Island. Violet Parker. I've met her all of two times in my sixteen years of life, but she never forgets to send me birthday and Christmas cards with money in them.

It takes Jose a while to find her number. Then he calls her. Maria sits there with her arm around my shoulders. Guadalupe's normal dark face is paler than I've ever seen it, and she doesn't say a word, not one word.

My knees are tucked up to my chin, and I'm resting

my head against the fish aquarium. My hair is stuck to my cheek and coming out of its braid. Jose's sitting on the floor in front of me, his back barely touching my legs, but he's there.

It's hard to breathe.

We wait for what seems like forever. No one comes to update me. I'm sick to my stomach. My throat is closed up, and I can't seem to breathe normally. Why are they taking so long?

Then, like an echo reverberating in a tunnel, a woman calls my name in a voice with a coarse edge to it. "Eleanor Martinson?" she asks again.

I have to focus hard to remember who I am. I can barely get my vocal cords to work. "Yeah, that's me." I slowly lift my head.

She clears her throat. "Do you remember me?" Her light brown hair is frizzy with curls about her face, and her clothes are wrinkled like she threw on whatever she could find. She's probably in her forties. She's carrying around a few extra pounds, although she's not fat.

"It's kind of hard to forget the only relative you've ever met." My voice is sharper than I mean it to be.

My mom hated my aunt. At least she hated how Aunt Violet always tried to help us, which is why I've never spent any time with my aunt.

I sit up, straighten my shirt, and try to smooth down my frizzing hair.

She tucks her bag tighter into her arms. "Thank you for calling." Her words are quiet, resigned, like the wind's been knocked out of her. She stares at me for another moment, and her chest rises and falls. "Listen, Eleanor, I just spoke with the doctor. I'm sorry to have to tell you this, but..."

Before she can get the words out, I hang my head but lift my gaze enough to meet her eyes, and say, "She's dead."

three days later

Things are foggy after that: fuzzy and chaotic. They officially diagnose my mom's death as an accidental drug overdose. I sit in my silent haze, letting them think whatever they want. I know the truth. She was careful in her drug use. She took just enough to take the edge off, but not enough to permanently harm her. That, in and of itself, is crazy, because they tell us every year in health class how drugs fry your brain. But my mom wasn't a stupid druggie – she was a sad one – and there's a difference.

Violet tries to talk to me, the cops try to talk to me, and the social services psychiatrist tries to talk to me. I don't want to talk. I have nothing to say.

A few days later, Violet and Guadalupe pretty much go at it. Guadalupe wants me to live in the trailer with them. But my aunt says *no*. She tells Guadalupe that even though they are probably like family to me, I have a real family on Orcas Island who loves me and will take care of me. She adds all this stuff about how I need to find my roots and discover where I've come from.

Guadalupe glares at her. Her English is broken, so when she gets real upset she goes off in Spanish. One of her kids has to translate for her. Maria does her best.

I'm determined to stay with the Lopez family. I have no desire to uproot my life and spend my last year of high school on some cold island in the middle of nowhere to discover a family my mom didn't even like. I fold my arms around myself to silently signal I'm not going.

Jose and Maria have gone to my trailer every day to get my stuff, but today they're going to throw it all in a suitcase. Violet and I are sitting at Guadalupe's kitchen table, waiting for them to come back with my things. I've taken to being silent around my aunt. Most people are uncomfortable with silence, and I'm doing my best to make her think I'm weird so she'll leave me alone. It's not working. She sits there at the table with me and smiles every once in a while.

I finally give in and talk to her. "I know you and Guadalupe have been talking about me going to Orcas Island. But I want to stay here with them. They're my family. Always have been."

She nods, and her eyes wrap me up with an I-know-you-think-so gaze. She says gently, "You can have family in more than one part of the world, you know."

I shake my head and stare at my hands. I twirl the silver rings on my pointer finger. "You can't create family out of nowhere. I don't even know you."

"That's the whole point. I'd like us to get to know each other. I'm not asking for forever. Why don't you try it for a few months?"

"I said no." I stand, pour a cup of the morning's coffee into a mug, and warm it in the microwave. When it's finished, I throw in some leftover milk that's on the table. I sip, my back against the counter, and force myself to look over at my aunt.

I grip my coffee mug. "It's not that I don't like you or anything. It's that I don't want to leave here. This is my home. I'm comfortable here."

She turns around in her chair. "I realize what I'm asking you to do is hard, but I'd like you to see where your mom grew up, get to know your cousins, the farm. You might come to like it."

"Thanks, Violet. But no." I walk back to Jose's room and close the door. Subject closed. Or so I think.

A few minutes later, Maria and Jose show up. The floor shakes as they drop my suitcase onto the rug. Low and muffled voices come from the living room. I can't make out much of what they're saying until Jose says, "Let me talk to her."

He walks back to his room and opens the door. I'm sitting on his bed drinking my coffee. I stare hard at him. "You don't think I should go with her, do you?" I pinch my lips together.

His eyes are shiny with tears. "Ellie, she really wants you to go with her."

I make a face like he's out of his mind. "I'm not going to that island. I'm not leaving you guys."

He takes hold of my shoulder and points around the trailer. "Look around you. There's nothing here for you. This trailer park isn't going anywhere, and both of us know you won't either if you stay here. You have dreams, things you want to do. You're smart. Maybe your aunt can help."

"I don't need her help."

His eyes narrow, and he cups my cheeks in his hands. "Yes you do, Ellie, and we both know it. How are you going to get to college and become a somebody living here?"

I stare down at the orange carpet. My whole world is this trailer park. I know who I am here. I hate it, but at least I know where I fit. There's also a part of me that's afraid to walk away from my mom. I know she's not in the trailer anymore. I know she's gone, but I can't leave her. "I'm scared."

He wraps his arms around me and whispers, "Just try

it out. We'll still be here."

I breathe in his familiarity and nod, but can't imagine leaving him, leaving my whole world. "I'll think about it." That's what I say, but I don't want to leave. In my mind, there's nothing to think about.

Violet won't let up, though. My mom was one of the most weak-willed women I've ever known, and Violet is like her complete opposite. Violet must have inherited all the willpower in the family because she's strong in a different way than anyone I've ever known. It comes from deep inside her.

A few days later, when she talks with the school counselor, Ms. Chatterson says it'll be fine for me to end my junior year early "considering the circumstances."

Ms. Chatterson leans across her desk far enough that I can see her cleavage, then sets her glasses on the tip of her nose, and peers over them. She talks to my aunt with one of those whispery voices that make me want to throw up. "As long as you promise to take good care of our Eleanor. She means the world to us, you know."

Violet tucks her purse tighter into her lap and raises an eyebrow. I get the feeling she's just as annoyed by Ms. Chatterson as I am. She reaches across the table and pats the counselor on the hand. "She means the world to a lot of people."

three weeks after

At the beginning of May, I move in with my aunt and uncle. I agreed to stay on Orcas Island for the summer. If by the end of August, I don't like living with them, I can go back to the trailer park. Violet will even drive me.

Their farm is nothing like what I expect. It doesn't fit any mold I've seen anywhere. They have three kids: Prissy, age six, and Gabe and Mikey, four-year-old twins. They also have a horse named Goldie, two bunnies, one guinea pig, and three cats. It's a lot. Supposedly, the white farmhouse has been in my family for three generations.

Violet's got something to say about everything. She's always muttering and talking to herself, and she's the most cluttered person I've ever known. She has stacks of stuff lying all over – half-finished scrapbooks, family albums in every bookcase, magazines piled up from five years ago. I still can't believe she and my mom were sisters. She's domestic to the extreme. My mom didn't even believe in putting a picture on the wall. Violet's got a garden bigger than my single-wide with every vegetable you can imagine, and a flower garden on the east side of the house. She sells fruits and vegetables at the farmer's market where she wears a straw hat and calls everyone by name.

Ben, on the other hand, doesn't say more than five words in a day. He drives a big blue pickup that's noisier than a tractor. He's broad and strong like my aunt's voice, but also tender. Sometimes when we're eating together at the table, I'll feel someone staring at me. It's usually Ben, and when I realize he's looking at me, he smiles and goes back to eating his food. I get the feeling he doesn't know what to do with a teenage girl, but he seems accepting of people regardless of who they are.

At first nothing really happens on the island. It rains. I sit around doing whatever my aunt says. I work in the garden, take care of the kids. I'm determined to earn my keep, and keep my distance. I don't want to get attached.

I'm normally the kind of person who can pull it together, but I'm haunted. I stare off into the air and have no idea what I'm even looking at. Sometimes it takes me ten minutes to dry one dish. Eventually Violet takes it from my hands and sets it in the cupboard.

At night, I hate going to bed. I curl into a ball and try hard to disappear. The first face I see whenever I drift off to sleep is my mom's. I startle and have to begin the whole process over again. Sometimes, I start shivering and can't stop. I sit, huddled on the bed trying to force all the images into the distant darkness. They won't get out of my head. I see myself arguing with my mom, Jose punching the wall. I even see Jazz grabbing my money. I see my mom's body.

God, it's hard to breathe.

I'm homeless and lost. As if I'm floating through dense fog, I can't see where I'm going anymore. Jose is working for a landscaping company, and because it's summer, he has no free time. He can hardly respond to my texts, let alone talk to me on the phone. We try to talk late at night when he's driving home from work, but it's not the same, and something about his distance forces the reality of my situation to crash in on me. I'm alone. At least I feel alone. There's no escaping it. Being in this new place, at this house with my happy little cousins who laugh and play like there's nothing wrong with the world, is more than I can handle. There's no way I'm going to make it here.

One night, a couple weeks after I arrive on the island, I'm sitting on my bed. Can't sleep. My hands grip my knees, pulling myself in as tightly as possible, rocking back and forth. The darkness closes around me, and I can't shake my way out of its grip. It's hard to swallow. My heart races. My throat is closing up. My chest is so tight it hurts. Jose isn't answering his phone. I've called him ten times, but it goes to voice mail. He's the only one who can pierce through the fog.

She's gone. My mom is gone. It's my fault. All my fault.

The farmhouse is full of space and air, there's life everywhere – in the kids' laughter, in my Aunt Violet's smile and laugh, in the flowers blooming. Even the trees are budding with flowers. It's suffocating. I can't help but think that my maybe my mom was right. Maybe it's easier to go to sleep and never wake.

On impulse, I grab the bottle of aspirin on my nightstand. I have allergy medicine in my suitcase. If I combine them, I could fall asleep and not wake up. And right now, I'd like nothing more than to escape the pain, the constant nagging thought that it's all my fault.

I grip the smooth, round bottle of pills – painkillers, to be exact. It's almost full. I pour about fifty pills into my hand. They're overflowing in my palm, a tiny mountain of pain relief. They intermingle, and I rub my fingers over their gritty texture. I'm shaking, shivering. My forehead is drenched in sweat. My tongue is thick. I still can't swallow.

I rock back and forth, back and forth, trying to muster up the courage to throw the handful of pills into my mouth, desperate to feel better, aching for escape.

A few tears leak from my eyes. I swipe them with the back of my hand, my fist clenched over the pills. I'm holding the painkillers so tightly, the rings on my fingers bite into my flesh. The rings. Seven of them, symbolizing wholeness. Something I'll never be again.

I can't do it.

I shove them back into the bottle and toss the bottle back into the nightstand drawer. I clear my throat and force myself out of my bed. Raking my hands through my hair, I walk to the window seat.

It's clear outside. The stars are shining brightly against the darkness above me. I sit there, staring up at the sky, trying to convince myself to give it a few more days. Not even that. I only have to make it through the night.

Just keep breathing, I tell myself. *All you have to do is breathe.*

the next morning

I'm not sure when I fall asleep, but I do. Against the window, staring up at the night sky.

In the morning, my neck has a crick, and my cheek is pressed against the cool glass.

Voices seep up through the floor, penetrating my grogginess. My aunt and uncle are talking in the bedroom below. After a few minutes of trying to ignore their hushed voices, I hear my name. It startles me.

Curious, I tiptoe down to the second floor. I huddle at the foot of the stairs and hide behind their partially open door.

Ben's pacing the floor. "Maybe she should go back to her friend's house, Vi. She's not happy. She won't talk about it. It may not have been right, us asking her to come here for the summer."

"Let's give her some more time," Violet says. "I've waited too long to know her. I don't want to give up yet. She'll come around. This island is in her blood."

"Violet, you should at least try to talk to her."

"I don't want to push her until she's ready. She needs to grieve. And this is a good place to do that. At least she isn't having to work like a grown woman to make rent."

I flinch. How did she know that?

"Well, how long is she going to grieve?" Ben asks.

"She's going to grieve until she's done grieving. It's only been a few weeks."

"She's so sad, Violet. I don't like to see her this sad. She seems so old. Older than she really is, like she's had to live through too much."

My aunt lets out a deep sigh. "I know, but can't you see how strong she is? The girl has resilience. She'll come around. Let's give her some space and see how she adjusts. If I force her to talk before she's ready, she'll leave. She doesn't trust us yet."

The bed creaks, and Ben's voice comes out muffled. "Nobody should have to deal with what she's lived through."

"But she did. We can't erase it, Ben. We can only give her love and time."

"What if she goes too deep into her darkness?" he asks.

I shiver. That darkness he's talking about is a force with claws, closing all around me.

"We'll watch her. She'll be all right. I've got a good feeling about her."

A hot tear trickles down my cheek. I brush it away. I've never heard anyone talk like that before, especially about me. As I hide at the foot of the stairs, with my throat closed up, I realize these people, whom I hardly know, might actually care about me – for real. Warmth tingles through me. I scurry back to my room. There's no way they could love me that much. It's too hard to believe. I hardly even know them.

I need to be alone.

seven weeks after june

The island warms up, and the fresh summer winds carry with them a calming, a strength that whispers to me, and surprisingly, an inkling to explore the island blows through my mind. After lunch, when I'm gazing out the window, I mention it to my aunt. She points outside to their horse, Goldie, in the orchard.

"She's a nice mare. You're free to ride her whenever you want."

I stand there for a second. "Are you serious?"

"Sure am," she says. "I should have said something about it before. You have at it."

I set my plate on the counter, open the farmhouse door, and go into the pasture. Goldie raises her head as I walk over to her. She nuzzles against me, rubbing her nose on my arm. I close my eyes, letting her get as close as she can.

Violet shows me where the horse tack is and says I should use a bareback riding pad. She explains that if you learn to ride bareback, you can ride anything, anytime. I question her logic when I'm falling off about a hundred times, but eventually I figure it out and start riding all over the place.

One afternoon, I'm on Goldie, wandering around by the edge of the cliffs. I wear a pair of cut-off jean shorts and flip-flops, my hair's hanging loose. I breathe in the fresh air and give myself permission to not feel guilty for five minutes. I pretend it's all different, that it's not the nightmare it really is, when I notice an old man off in the distance. He seems to be watching me. Then he turns around and vanishes.

I urge Goldie farther down the path to find him, and that's when I discover it: a cottage lighthouse, hidden behind a grove of trees on the edge of a high rocky cliff.

It's faded white with tall grass growing all around it, and it has a rustic, red door. At the top, the light is surrounded by a circular porch. The shutters are broken off their hinges and dangle in the air. It almost brings tears to my eyes, discarded and empty as it is. I nudge Goldie toward it. For a few moments, I get lost in everything around me and forget to breathe. I forget what happened to my mom. I forget what I said to her. I'm just here. Right now. In this moment.

The wind lifts my hair, swirling it around my neck. Blue sky hovers over me, strong and vast. The waves swish against the rocks below. The warm salt air smells clean and hopeful. Something stirs deep inside of me.

I dismount, still holding the reins, and walk to the nearest window. I wipe off some of the grime with the edge of my shirt. Inside, the furniture is shrouded in white sheets. Bookshelves stand erect and lofty off to one side. A spiral staircase ascends to crow's nest.

All of a sudden the hair on my arms stands up. Someone's looking at me. I turn around and mount Goldie.

Then, out of nowhere, a black dog comes running from the cliffs. She lunges at Goldie's heels, snapping and snarling. Goldie spooks, jumping to the right. I tumble off.

The dog paces back and forth, still growling. I stay crouched and inch my way back. Her stomach is bulging as if she's pregnant. Her dark coat is caked with mud. Her eyes are mad white.

I reach for Goldie's reins. She swerves, tosses her head, and paws the ground, trying to protect me. In one swift move, I stand, grab a handful of mane, and leap on. I pull on the reins, turning Goldie's head toward the path, and gallop off. The dog follows us, nipping at the horse's hooves. Goldie breaks into a trot, and the dog falls behind.

Before I'm completely out of sight, I turn around and call, "I'll be back to help you."

At the farmhouse, I don't say anything about the dog, but straightaway, I ask Violet about the lighthouse.

"You found the lighthouse, huh?" she says, her back to me. She's kneading bread and wearing her neon pink apron. Her whole body rocks back and forth. The heels of her thick, tough hands shove the dough up and down on the wooden table like she's a wrestler. Her bread is amazing. I can't wait until the homey smell fills the house. One more way Violet's drastically different from my mom. It's like living on a television sitcom – the ones I'd convinced myself didn't exist.

I grab an apple from the fruit bowl on the table. "It looks pretty abandoned. Does the lighthouse belong to someone here on the island?"

"Actually, it belongs to our family." Violet brushes the hair out of her face, and a smidge of flour sticks to her forehead. "We haven't gone near it for ages, though. Your mom used to go up there.

My mom went to the lighthouse?

"I never cared much for it," she says. "It felt haunted, like someone was watching me. Rose didn't think so. Sometimes I'd search for hours to find her, then sure enough, she'd be up there in the crow's nest, staring at the water."

Violet cuts the dough in pieces and shapes the loaves.

"My grandfather was a sailor. He'd go out to sea for months. His wife, Eleanor, built that lighthouse so she could light his way home every night." She lifts her head. "That's who you're named after."

I keep my face serious to hide my surprise. "My mom never told me that." I never knew anything about my family. She hadn't told me anything about this island either. I sit on the table and rest my cheek on the palm of my hand.

Violet pauses. Her face turns dark, like a shadow passes over it. "I'm sure she didn't." She hesitates as if she wants to say more, but decides to keep it inside.

I take a big bite of the apple, and it cracks in the air. My aunt puts the bread in the oven, then she turns to me with her serious stare. Sometimes I think she can read people's minds.

"You can go into the lighthouse if you want. The key is inside the porch light. Be careful of rats and stuff, but feel free to check it out."

I take a deep breath. "OK" is all I say. Something's pulling me toward that lighthouse, beckoning me to search inside. Maybe if I go inside, go somewhere my mom used to be, it'll help me figure out what happened to her. What happened to me.

My whole life, my mom was seriously sad. Sad in a different way than most people. She'd lie on the couch and not get up, lost in space somewhere. Not moving. Not blinking. Sometimes, she'd stay in bed all day and smoke until it looked like morning fog in her bedroom. I could ask my aunt about her. But I don't.

Maybe I don't want to hear the truth yet.

a trip to town

The next morning, I'm lying in bed trying to fall back asleep when one of the twins opens my door. I still can't tell which is which. He's licking a big purple lollipop. I'm positive Violet didn't give it to him, but he's sucking on that round ball like he's never had anything sweet before. Purple streaks of slobber cover his face, from hairline to chin. He beelines for the bed and wraps his sticky hand around my arm.

"Ellie?" he says. "Are you awake? I'm hungry."

I hide my face in my pillow, wishing I could sleep one more hour, but I sort of like that he came upstairs to see me. "Give me a few more minutes."

"Come on." He tugs on my arm, points to the door. "Ellie, please." He rubs his tummy.

I moan. I won't be able to go back to sleep. "All right, let's go."

Once I'm in the kitchen, I drop some toast into the toaster, put orange juice in a green plastic cup, and sit beside him. I squint at him. "Are you Gabe?"

He smiles. "No, I'm Mikey." He puts his finger on his chest and puffs himself up.

I grin, and he bursts out laughing.

Mikey chats about his favorite truck and how his dad is going to teach him to ride a bike without training wheels, and I don't even hear the knock on the door.

Alex," Mikey shouts.

"Who?" I ask, turning toward the door.

Mikey shakes his head and gives me a don't-you-know-anything-stare. "Alex. He lives next door.

I think Violet introduced me to him a couple weeks ago. "Does he mow the lawn for your dad?"

Mikey nods, then motions to Alex. "Come in."

Alex steps inside and closes the door behind him. I give him a half smile and take a moment to actually see him. I'm completely checked out, I've hardly noticed anything these days. He's redheaded with a million freckles that cover every last inch of his face. He's kind of cute.

"Hi, Ellie. How's it going?"

I smooth down my hair. "Hey. It's good. Don't you mow lawns or something?"

"Yes. I'm a landscaper. I have my own summer business."

Since when did mowing lawns become landscaping?

Mikey points to Alex. "He's the best soccer player on the island. Except for Will."

"Who's Will?" I ask, pouring Mikey some orange juice.

Alex fiddles with a set of keys sitting on the counter. "He's Julie's son."

"Who?"

Mikey shakes his head again. "Julie. Mom's friend. Don't you remember?"

Barely. I think she owns a coffee house on the island. She and Violet are close. Violet's tried to drag me into town to introduce me to people, but I haven't wanted to go. I'm not some trophy on display. No matter what Violet thinks.

"I think he and Amy are coming in today."

Alex is staring at me. I glance down at my shirt, making sure I haven't spilled anything. I clear my throat to show him that I'm waiting for him to tell me why he's here.

He turns partway to the door and gestures outside. "I need to go into town. Ben wants me to pick up something at the general store."

Mikey's eyes brighten. "Can I go with you?"

Alex nods. "Fine with me."

Mikey turns to me. "You come too, Ellie."

I don't think that's a good idea. "I should help with breakfast."

"Come on," Alex says. "I'll introduce you to Amy. Like I said, I think she and Will got in last night."

I clear Mikey's plate from the table. "Why do I want to meet Amy?"

"She's our age. Will's a couple years older." He raises his eyebrows. "And has a lot of problems."

"Oh, really?"

"He got kicked out of his school back in Seattle. They had to put him in some all-boys private school. But Amy's great. I think you'll like her." Alex opens the farmhouse door. "Are we going or what?"

I wipe Mikey's face with a rag. I tell Alex I'll be right back and then glance toward the foot of the kitchen stairs. "Does Violet have a wagon or stroller we could put him in?"

"Yeah, I'll grab it out of the garage."

I run upstairs to my room, grab my phone, and go back to the middle-floor bathroom to brush my teeth and braid my hair. I tiptoe by Prissy's room, trying not to wake her, but as I pass her door, she sits up in bed, rubbing her eyes. "Where're you going?"

"To town with Alex and Mikey." I take a couple steps back and rest against the doorframe. "Alex has to buy something for your dad, and Mikey wants to go along.

We're taking him in the wagon." Before I know it, I add, "You want to come?"

Prissy jumps out of bed, throws off her pajamas, and starts getting dressed. "I'll be right down."

"We'll get Mikey in the wagon and meet you outside."

I creep down the stairs, hoping Gabe won't want to join us. Where in the world is Violet? She never sleeps in. She's usually awake before the sun. I leave her a note so she won't worry.

When I step out the door, Gabe is sitting next to Mikey in the wagon with a matching lollipop in his mouth and a bright grin.

Alex smiles when I step out the door. He eyes the twins. "This should be interesting."

"Tell me about it. Prissy's coming too." I can't believe I'm going into town with all the kids and the neighbor who calls himself a landscaper.

Alex stares at me some more. I try to think of something to say, but stand there in awkward silence until Prissy runs out of the house in a pink sundress with flowers on it, an apple in one hand, a five dollar bill in the other, and her hair wild.

"I'll pull the wagon," she says, shoving her money into a small pocket on the front of her sundress and taking a bite of apple.

"All right. But if you want to eat your apple, that's fine too."

"I can do both."

Prissy takes the prize for bossy older sister. She's going into second grade. And never stops talking. Never.

Alex paces ahead of us. I walk next to Prissy, who's doing a good a pretty good job with the wagon, but after a few minutes, I take over so she can chomp on her apple and tell me about everything we pass.

The farmhouse is about a mile from town, and it takes us at least half an hour to walk there. The road is long and straight with big farmhouses on one side, woods on the other. In the distance, people are watering their gardens, and cows graze in the open pastures. Finally, we come to a slight bend in the road with large cherry trees on either side and a slight downhill slope. At the bottom, the town comes into view.

Alex explains that Orcas Island is divided into three groups – the locals, families who have vacationed on this island for years, and frustrated artists trying to make their way in the world. "The frustrated artists aren't hard to miss." He pushes up the sleeves of his sweatshirt, because the morning sun is warming up the island. "They carry thick canning jars of coffee everywhere, doing their part to save the planet, I guess."

As we roll onto Main Street, Gabe and Mikey start fighting.

Mikey yelps. "Ellie, Gabe hit me."

"Because he wouldn't move over. He's taking up the whole wagon."

I pat Gabe's head. "We'll be there in a minute," I tell them. "Try to be nice to each other."

Most of the houses around Main Street have that beachy, rustic look about them, with blue shingles and cute white fences. The town's not exactly hopping or anything. There's Julie's Café, a few clothing stores, one small bookstore, and one or two restaurants. The sidewalks are wooden, and a short, white picket fence runs along one side.

Alex walks beside me and takes Prissy's hand while I pull the wagon.

We stop by the café before Alex goes to the hardware store. He opens the door so I can get the twins inside. It's hard to get the wagon through the door. Alex helps me pick it up and tilt it to the side. The boys laugh like they're on a roller-coaster. We manage to jam it through. Inside the café, I keep the boys buckled in the wagon. If they escape, I'll never get them back.

I get them situated off to one side and admire the

antique wood floors, the rustic wooden tables, and the benches lining the large picture window that faces Main Street. Croissants and pastries fill the glass case, and a girl is working behind the counter. People are sitting in every available space in the room, and the enticing smells of fresh ground coffee, cinnamon, and vanilla linger in the air.

Another girl, sitting behind the register, is about my age with gorgeous blonde hair. The kind that you wish were fake, but it's not. And a smattering of freckles across her nose so perfectly placed they look dotted on by a Hollywood make-up artist.

She smiles when we come through the door. "Hey, Alex. Good to see you."

Alex waves at her. Before he can introduce me, our glances meet.

"Hi! You must be Eleanor?" She hands someone a croissant and latte, and thanks him for coming in.

I nod, fake a smile. "Everyone calls me Ellie."

"I'm Amy. People just call me Amy." She grins like it's a hilarious joke.

"So you work here?" I ask.

"I help my mom. My brother and I switch off shifts all summer. In Seattle, I don't have to work, especially not at five in the morning."

"Where's Will?" Alex asks.

Amy shrugs. "Beats me. He was supposed to be here an hour ago." She rings up a muffin for a customer at the counter. "How long are you in town for, Ellie?" Amy asks.

"Till the end of August. Then I go back home."

She sets her arm on the counter and rests her chin on the palm of her hand. Her hair falls over her shoulders, cascading over her shirt and onto the counter. I almost reach out and touch it. It's like Cinderella hair, and I want to make sure it's real.

"Maybe we could hang out sometime," she says. "My mom and your aunt are really good friends."

I turn away from her golden locks and force myself to focus. "Sure." I hope she doesn't ask me for a specific time or anything.

"Great. When?"

Guess not. My gaze darts around the coffee shop. "Whenever, I guess."

She frowns just enough to show a hint of disappointment. She lowers her voice, "When I have plans, my mom has more leverage with Will. He's almost eighteen and hates this island, pretty much hates just about everything in life, except his books and girls."

As much as I'd like to disappear and pretend that there are no people in this world, that I can live my life without anyone, I can't. Jose would tell me I need to come out of my cave and make a friend. I take a deep breath. "How about tomorrow around ten? We can go shopping or something."

"Perfect." Her blue eyes sparkle. "I'll meet you here. Oh, and it's the Fourth of July. We always go to the fireworks show. You should come."

I stiffen. I can handle a couple hours of shopping. I'm not sure I can do all day. "I don't know what Violet's planning. But I'll check with her."

Mikey pinches Gabe on the leg.

"Ouch!" Gabe slaps him hard in the arm.

Mikey screeches.

I have to get out of here.

Alex steps forward. "Um, Ellie, maybe I should take Gabe to the store. And you can keep Mikey and Prissy with you."

Before I can say anything, Amy takes off her apron. "I'll go with you, Alex. I was hoping to talk to you about something. Will's supposed to be here any minute."

His eyebrows furrow, but he shrugs. "Sure."

She starts following him, but then turns to me. "Ellie, I'll be right back."

They walk out of the café, and I'm left with Prissy and

Mikey and the wagon. I ask Prissy to watch Mikey while I order a grande vanilla latte. I hand the girl some money, and wait while she's making it.

A loud bang makes me jump. Prissy's trying to push the wagon outside. But the tire's jammed in the door. People are waiting outside, trying to get in.

The girl hands me my latte. I grab it and rush to the door. I take the wagon handle and give Prissy the latte.

But the wagon won't fit through the door. I decide to go at it from the other direction. It's too clunky, and without Alex it's heavy. Why did I agree to come here in the first place? I can't stand chaos. I step onto the wagon, maneuver around Mikey, and land on the other side, outside the café.

Back turned, I hunch over to push the wagon back out of the way. I bump someone behind me. "Sorry," I say without turning.

"Wagons and strollers aren't allowed inside." The voice from behind startles me.

My cheeks flame. "I. Was. Just. Leaving."

I lift the wagon and tilt it slightly to get it out the door. Then I jerk it past the person I bumped. I almost trip into the street. I peek over my shoulder to get a better look at the guy.

Our eyes lock, and I take a deep breath. His eyes are the color of the Caribbean water, and he's looking at me with a piercing clarity. When I realize I'm full-on staring, I force my gaze back to Prissy and mumble something about asking for help the next time she decides to leave the café.

Even though the wagon is now on the sidewalk, and we're no longer blocking the entrance, the guy stays outside. When the tension is thick enough that I wonder if I'll ever be able to take another deep breath, Alex shows up with Amy.

"Finally, Will," Amy says. "I've been waiting for you to get here for over an hour."

as waters gone by

This gorgeous guy is Amy's brother? Just perfect. His blonde hair is scruffy and messed up in that product sort of way, and he has earrings in both ears.

"What's going on here?" he says. "It's a crazy show, and you just disappear?"

"You're late."

"And that gives you permission to leave the café? And since when did we start letting strollers and wagons in here?"

"This is Ellie," she says, ignoring his question.

Amy points to her brother and makes a disgusted face. "Ellie, this is my brother, Will. The one I told you about."

I raise one eyebrow and give a curt nod, "Hey," is all I say, trying hard to act disinterested, but I'm intrigued, despite his rude behavior. "We should go," I tell Alex. "I'll see you tomorrow, Amy." I ignore her brother.

We ramble home. Prissy chats with the twins and pulls the wagon. Alex and I walk next to each other. "How long have you known Amy?" I ask as we approach the farmhouse.

"Since we were kids. Before her parents got divorced, they used to come here every summer and on long weekends to their family's beach house."

I leave it there, but wonder about their parents' divorce. And I'm not sure I want to hang out with Amy. What if she asks me about my mom? That makes me ill. I've decided to tell everyone that my mom was sick. No details. I don't need to tell anyone the truth. Weird looks and pity comments aren't going to make it better. Besides, I'm leaving at the end of the summer. Who cares if no one knows the truth.

We wander down the driveway and leave the wagon at the foot of the porch stairs. I'm not taking that thing back into town anytime soon.

When we open the kitchen door, the smell of sweet cinnamon and melted butter wafts out. My stomach growls. Violet, in her pink apron, is washing dishes in the kitchen sink. Ben is standing behind her, his hands on her waist, kissing her neck. We all stop in the doorway, and the boys giggle and point. Alex blushes the color of his hair. I try to look away from Violet and Ben, but I can't. There's a security about their relationship I've never seen before.

Ben takes the plates off the counter and starts setting the table. Violet pulls fresh cinnamon rolls from the oven. She smothers the top with white frosting and sets them on the table with fresh fruit and orange juice. We sit down and pass the steaming rolls.

A few minutes later, Ben asks Alex whether he got the tool.

"Yeah, I bought it." Alex stuffs another huge bite into his mouth.

"Who was working at Julie's?" Violet asks.

Prissy answers, "Amy was there waiting for Will, but then Ellie bumped into him. Will was mean to her."

Violet reaches for the orange juice. "I'm not surprised," she mutters. "Did you like Amy?"

"I guess." I reach for the juice after she fills her cup. "We're getting together tomorrow. She's going to show me around. Unless you have some work for me to do."

I try to help out while I'm staying here. I don't want handouts. I break off a piece of cinnamon roll and place it in my mouth. And the warm dough melts on my tongue.

Gabe and Mikey are both devouring their cinnamon rolls. I haven't heard a word from them since we sat down.

"No, I don't have any work for you to do. I'm glad you met Amy. Julie was hoping you'd become friends."

"She seems nice." I give my aunt a half grin.

Violet sips her orange juice. "She is nice. Her family has gone through a terrible ordeal the past few years, and that girl has born the brunt of it."

I decide not to ask about the terrible ordeal. Instead, I nod politely and ask, "How much does she work at the cafe?"

Ben speaks up. "More than any young girl should have to on her summer vacation." Like he wants to make sure I know they don't want me working through my vacation. "And Will works a lot too," he says. "He's angry and gets in trouble, but he'd do anything for his mom. Will's been mad at the world since his parents divorced."

Ben leaves it there. Even though I want to ask more, I decide not to. Sometimes people shouldn't ask.

I help Violet clean up breakfast. Then we work in the garden for an hour. I pull weeds, digging into the moist soil, and scour the bed for vegetables that are ready. There's something calming about a vegetable garden. I always wanted to have one in the trailer park, but we didn't have room.

Finally Violet says, "Don't you want to go to the lighthouse?"

I try to mask my excitement. "Yeah, but I can work some more."

"You've been itching to see that lighthouse since we talked about it yesterday. Skedaddle. Think you'll make it back for dinner?"

"Sure."

I dust off my hands and shorts, and bring my vegetable basket over to Violet. Just before I leave the garden, Violet touches my arm, and I turn around. She throws her arms around me and gives me one of the biggest hugs I've ever had. She runs her hand over my hair and holds me tight. I don't think she's going to say anything, but then she grips my shoulders and pulls back until she can see into my eyes.

"I'm glad you're here." She has tears in her eyes. "You bring a great deal to this family."

I pat her a couple of times on the arm, shift my weight from side to side. Her tenderness is hard to bear. I can't stay near it for long. It's as if her caring forces everything up to the surface. It's easier to stay on the outskirts. It's almost as if her kindness calls to me, whispers in my ear that it's safe to feel my pain. But it's a lie. It's not safe, because nothing can make what I did OK. I want it to disappear.

Violet must sense my discomfort, because she releases her hold, giving me my space again.

"Go on, Ellie," she says, patting my cheek. "Have a good afternoon. But be careful."

"Thanks." I run out of the yard before she gets all sentimental again.

I head back into town first to see if the bookstore has anything on lighthouses and crazy dogs. It's a long shot, but I'm a sucker for small bookstores. I buy some dog food, hoping to woo the black dog.

Walking down Main Street, I pass a consignment store with a cool vintage look. I like to wear clothes other people wouldn't normally put together. I've become a master at saving money and figuring out how to make it work on a next to zero budget. Some people say I look like a hippie. Maybe's it's my long dark curly hair that I keep in a tight braid down my back. Or maybe it's that I don't usually wear makeup.

My mom wore a lot of makeup, and I always felt like the real Rose was hiding underneath all the crap she put on her face. I never wanted to hide. At least not my face. My past is a different matter. I have a long list about life in the trailer park I keep locked up.

I bump into Amy and her mom on my way down the street. Amy squints like she trying to figure something out.

"Hey," I say and shuffle my bag around.

"Weren't you just here?" She points to the café.

"Yeah, but I forgot to get something." I hope she doesn't offer to come shopping with me.

Her mom grins at me. Julie must be about Aunt

Violet's age, but her blue eyes seem sad and worn, like she's cried a lot. Although, like Will's, they're crystal clear.

"Hi, Ellie. How are you these days?" Julie uses that tone people have when they know you've been through a tragedy. I study the dirt on the sidewalk for a second and swallow.

"I'm fine," I say real firm like. "Thanks for asking." I can only imagine what Aunt Violet has told her about my mom. I hope she doesn't tell Amy. The last thing I need is Amy's pity.

I glance down the sidewalk. "I have to go, but it was good to see you."

Amy seems as if she's going to ask to come along, but then she says, "Are we still getting together tomorrow?"

"Yeah. I'll meet you at the café in the morning."

Amy waves as I walk toward the bookstore, and I breathe a sigh of relief.

The smell of books welcomes me in. I ask the cashier where I can find information on dogs and anything on the history of Orcas Island. In particular, I ask if they have any books on lighthouses. She directs me, and after thanking her, I adjust my bag and head to the history section. I squeeze down one aisle, perusing different titles. I reach the end and stop suddenly. Amy's brother is slouched in a brown leather chair, engrossed in an old copy of the *Lord of the Rings: The Two Towers*.

I hope he doesn't notice me. I turn to go in the other direction, but my bag bangs the bookshelf.

Will sets the book in his lap. His eyes light up as he studies me. "Where's your little red wagon?"

I can't decide if he is being rude or funny. I push aside a curl that's escaped from my braid.

"Left it outside," I say. "Didn't want to risk rude management in another store today."

He raises his eyebrows. I squeeze past to search for the books. I'm sure he's staring at me, but I refuse to turn around. I must admit though, I'm unnerved. I also can't figure out why he's in the bookstore reading a copy of a book he clearly brought with him. Not to mention that I love the *Lord of the Rings*. The first time I read the trilogy, I was thirteen. Now, I read it every year.

The leather chair squeaks. Will gets up and walks over. "I know this bookstore from top to bottom. You need help finding something?"

"No, thanks." I turn my back and mutter, "I don't want to keep you from the Riders of Rohan."

He lifts one arm, rests it against the bookshelf, and stares at me.

I force myself to look at him.

"Ah...you've seen the movies?" he asks.

"Something like that." I pick up a book called *Lighthouses in the San Juan Islands* and flip through the pages.

He shifts his stance. "What's the deal with lighthouses?"

I close the book and tuck it under my arm. "Just curious about the island, I guess."

He goes back to his seat again and opens his book. He doesn't say anything until I have to pass his chair again. "So, why is some girl from the city looking for books on lighthouses?"

I lift one eyebrow. "Why is some *boy* sitting like a hermit in the farthest corner of a bookstore, reading a copy of an old book he most likely brought with him?"

His eyes widen, and he hesitates. I must have surprised him with my sass.

"I guess we're both stumped." Will leans back in the chair.

"I guess." I walk past him to the cash register and don't give myself permission to glance back.

I buy the book on lighthouses. I'll do online research for the dog information. I shove the book in my bag and walk to the trail.

The lighthouse emerges through the pockets of light in the woods. My pace quickens. Once I'm there, I pour some dog food into the bowl, set the bag on the lighthouse patio, and start the downward hike toward the water. Stiff edges of sun-scorched grass scrape my bare legs as I stumble down the cliff's steep trail. The dog's footprints wind down through the undergrowth to the water below. I slip on dry sand and trip on short tufts of grass. Grasping the tall reeds with one hand, I steady myself. Biting my bottom lip and clutching the plastic bowl, I inch down to the rocky ledge below.

Against the side of the cliff, a small cave catches my eye. The cave is dark, just the sort of place where a dog might hide. Crouching, I creep toward it as silently as possible.

The dog lurches out, growling and baring her teeth. My heart speeds up, and I edge back. Then I kneel, keeping a wary eye on her, and set the dog food down. "It's all right. I have some food for you." My voice tips on the brink of panic. "I'm not here to hurt you, girl."

She's pacing as if she's about to pounce. I need to get away, but I want to gain her trust. I finally leave the bowl just off the path. It's going to take a lot of work, but that dog needs someone to care about her. She needs some kindness in her life.

I climb back up to the lighthouse and reach up to get the key from the patio light. Cobwebs glaze the back of my hands, and my fingers brush against bug carcasses. I recoil, fighting the heebie-jeebies, and bump the cool metal of a key. I pull it out and rub off the dirt and grime on my shorts.

My fingers shake as they press the key into the lock. I wiggle it back and forth until it clicks.

I push the door open and let the musty smell of an old house that's been closed up for too long drift out. Bright light from the windows streams in making me shelter my eyes with my hand.

It's magic. The moment I step over the threshold, the cottage wraps itself around my tired, exhausted self and whispers its lullaby to my heart. Despite the grime, the dust, the musty odor, it's as if I've finally found a home. Not like in my trailer or even Jose's house, but home, like in the stories I've read, where there's no need to hide, no need to cover up. A place to rest, to be secure.

The large room, with a bed to the left and the living area near the door, is spacious, inviting me to put up my feet and let down my guard. The bookshelves and furniture covered in white sheets give it an old English feel, like stepping into a Jane Austen novel. Stories of people's lives linger in the air and leave a mysterious residue.

In the silence, the room unfolds around me, standing bare and open. I gasp when I see old copies of *Pride and Prejudice, Jane Eyre, Wuthering Heights,* and many other favorites lining the bookshelf. A miniature kitchen on the back wall has tall windows overlooking the cliff, beckoning in the ocean's light, and in the middle of the room, standing tall and unwavering, a dark, wrought iron, spiral staircase, wide enough for only one person to ascend, curves upward.

I tiptoe around not wanting to touch anything. As far as I can tell, there aren't any rat droppings, but it's filthy. The dust layer is at least an inch thick, and the floor is black from dirt in the corners. Cobwebs dangle from the ceiling.

The pitted metal on the staircase railing scratches my hand as I pull myself onto the bottom step and climb, one riser at a time, making sure none of them are broken. Despite their fragile appearance, the steps are solid.

I shove open the push door overhead, and warm salt-laced air blows into my face. Light streams down. Squinting to shield my eyes from such brightness, I pull myself up until I can stand upright outside. The circular balcony is just large enough for me to walk around.

The panoramic view goes for miles. Off in the horizon, ferries glide across the smooth waters into and around the islands.

I'm leaning against the black iron railing, absorbing everything surrounding me, and it comes like a flash. I know what I'm supposed to do this summer – restore the lighthouse. Energy charges through my mind. Out of the layers of sadness in the pit of my stomach, a gush of excitement rushes up and dances through me. Yes. A lighthouse restoration is perfect.

I climb down and make a mental list of everything the cottage needs. I scrape the wall, and a thick layer of dust comes off, leaving my fingers black with dirt. A good scrubbing, some window cleaner, a broom, and a fresh coat of paint will go miles in restoring its rustic beauty. Reluctantly, I step outside, lock the door, and drop the key back in the porch light.

As I step onto the patio, an old man comes over the ridge. "Hey! Who are you?" he yells. "What are you doing at this lighthouse?" He limps toward me.

I stumble back against the side of the cottage. I can't catch my breath. "Um...I just found it, that's all."

He shakes his cane at me. "You can't come here. It ain't your lighthouse."

My heart's racing as I try to figure out how to get around him and back to Violet's.

Then, his eyes dart all around as if he's looking for something. "Where's that crazy dog?"

"You know about the dog?"

"She's crazy. Don't go near her." His voice is rumbly, like he's smoked for years.

"She just needs a kind touch," I tell him, my voice searching for confidence. "Maybe too many people were mean to her."

He spits on the ground. "It don't matter what happened to that dog. Stay away from her. She ain't safe.

And stay away from this lighthouse. It's old. You shouldn't be hanging around it."

"Maybe you're right," I say, hoping to placate him, to escape. *God, I hope he didn't see me put the key back.* He could break in or even try to move in.

"I'd better get home." My palms are sweating. I zigzag past him and dash toward the trail as fast as I can. I run the whole way down it, glancing back every few seconds to make sure he isn't following me.

He's gone. *Poof.* Nowhere to be seen. My heart speeds up again. *What just happened?*

It takes me a few minutes to stop shaking and calm my breathing. Does Violet know who he is? I'm not going to say anything. The last thing I want is for her to tell me I can't go to the lighthouse because of some crazy old man. But what am I going to do about him?

4th of july

Overnight, a heat wave arrives. Crazy hot. The kind of hot where the air stands so stagnant and thick you can reach out and touch it.

When I leave the house in the morning, Violet is already filling the kids' swimming pool. I have on a pair of flip-flops, and I'm wearing a swimsuit underneath my cut-off jean shorts and tank top, because all I want to do is strip down and jump into the ocean.

Amy spots me when I'm coming down Main Street. Her eyes light up, and she waves at me with more enthusiasm in one hand than I have in my entire body. I half wave in response. Her hair is pulled back in a neckline ponytail, and she has on a blue sundress that matches her eyes. She's overly happy. Like one of those girls who act as if they've never have a bad day, but really, they just don't know how to tell you they're having a bad day, because they don't know how to be anything but perfect.

"Do you like to swim?" she asks when I get to Julie's Café.

I wipe the sweat from my brow and lift my gaze to the hot sun. "Please tell me you know where we can get cooled off."

"Did you bring your suit?"

I nod. I'm glad I have on my red bikini.

"Good." She points toward the road that goes to the ferry. "There's this really fun lake where a bunch of us go when it gets really hot." She reaches for the door to the café. "Do you want to see if Alex wants to come?" she asks.

I shrug. I don't care one way or the other. Maybe she thinks Alex and I are good friends or something.

The café is cool, and I breathe a sigh of relief. Julie's behind the counter taking some pastries out of the window. She smiles at us as we step inside.

People are clustered all over the place. Some are standing in line for coffee, some are waiting to be served, others are seated at the tables, and Will's off in a corner, still reading. He's now on book three, *The Return of the King*. He isn't very far in, but still, he's read a lot since the day before.

Almost as if he can feel someone staring at him, he glances up from his book, and our eyes meet – again. I'm tempted to turn away, but I stare him down, hoping he won't say anything snarky about a red wagon or lighthouse books. He doesn't, but instead gives me curt nod. I raise one eyebrow and nod back.

Amy stops to gives some instructions to the girl who's working the espresso maker, then says over her shoulder, "Hey, Ellie, could you call Alex for me? This might take a while."

I slide my phone out of my pocket. "What's his number?"

She tells me. I punch it in. I'm about to ask her what I should tell him when she says, "Let him know we're going to the lake."

I feel kind of stupid dialing his number. I've never called him before.

"Ellie?" he asks when he answers, sounding really excited that I've called.

I tell him I'm hanging out with Amy, and we're going to the lake soon.

When I hang up, I call to Amy, "He's with Jacob, and they're already on their way there."

"Oh, good." She's done helping with the expresso maker and is packing some chips in a bag. "I've known Alex since I was like five years old." She opens one of the refrigerator doors and pulls out some cold drinks. "So, have you met his friend Jacob?"

Names and faces are all a blur. I squint, trying to remember. "Do his parents run the bed and breakfast here in town?" I ask. "I think Alex hangs out with him a lot."

"Yeah, it's a pretty famous bed and breakfast," she says. "Have you met him?"

I shake my head.

"He's really good-looking."

Amy tells her mom we're going to the swimming hole, and then she glances at her brother. "Are you coming with us or what?"

He peers at Amy and then back at his book. I think he's trying to decide which is the better option. I'm tempted to tell him to stay with the book – it's more promising – but I stay quiet.

Amy puts her hand on her hip. "Nadine's coming."

He slowly closes his book, takes a deep breath, and stands.

When we step into the street, the warm air blasts us, and I take a deep breath. A girl with light brown hair and a dark tan heads toward us.

Amy waves. "Hey, Nadine," she calls. "You were supposed to be here an hour ago." She links her arm through mine. "This is Ellie."

Nadine turns and scans me. "Hey," she says. But before I can say anything, she turns to Will and stares at him like he's a rock star come to Orcas. Oh, please. I wouldn't give him the satisfaction.

Amy nudges me. "Don't worry about Will," she says. "He doesn't talk to anyone. Don't take it personally. All he wants to do is read his stupid books. I just don't get why he'd want to read that trilogy again. They made the movies. He should just watch them."

I shake my head. "Why in the world would you watch the movies, if you could read the books? You miss half the story in those movies."

Amy raises her arms in the air as if she's surrendering. "Well, at least someone can talk books with Will. I'm more of a visual learner myself."

I laugh. "I'll remember that, Amy."

Will has an odd look on his face. Surprise maybe? He wraps his arm around the new girl but locks eyes with me for a fleeting moment, and a connection deeper than words, an understanding, passes between us. A moment no one else even notices. Electricity tingles down my spine.

By the time we get to the lake, sweat glistens on every part of me. I just want to get in the water. Normally, I wouldn't get caught dead letting everyone see me in my bikini, but I'm too hot to care.

The entire island of middle school and high school kids must come here on a hot day. A stand of trees provides shade on one side. Kids are tanning on and jumping off two big docks. Some are splashing in the water, and others are sitting in the grassy field off to the side, smoking. A whiff of pot lingers in the air, and partially hidden by the trees, a group of kids are hanging out in a haze of smoke.

Amy lays down her bag, sprawls out on her towel, holds up the bottle of sunscreen, and asks me to put sun lotion on her. A tinge of annoyance shoots through me. I take off my tank top and shorts, aching to get into the water, but I slather Amy's back and shoulders.

"Want me to put lotion on your back, Ellie?"

"No, thanks. I don't really burn." I stand. The only

thing I want is to get out of the hot sun and swim. People around me are studying me, trying to figure out who I am, but my sixth sense warns me that someone is checking me out. I glance around, but don't spot anyone in particular. Will pulls off his shirt, and Nadine hands him her suntan lotion and lifts her hair for him rub it on her back. Must be my imagination.

I turn to Amy. "Are you ready?"

"I'm going to lie out in the sun first," she says. "I like to get really hot before I swim."

I shake my head in disbelief. That tinge of annoyance is no longer just a tinge. Amy is seriously not the kind of girl I normally hang out with.

"Well, I'm going in."

Everyone is using the dock as a diving board, and off in the distance, toward the middle of the lake, hangs a monstrous rope swing. A few guys are climbing the hill and swinging off it into the water. I veer past Will, who is rubbing sunscreen on Nadine's back, and dive in. The cool water sends tingles through my whole body. I swim under water, gliding toward the middle of the lake. I surface, wipe the water from my eyes, and smooth back my hair.

I flip onto my back and close my eyes, floating. The water is finally cooling down my internal temperature. It's so nice to not be sweltering. It also gives me a few moments to collect myself and release the tension bubbling inside me. After few minutes, two guys swim up next to me. I recognize Alex's bright red hair bobbing up and down in the water. The other guy has almost black hair and is staring at me as if I'm some odd fish he's never seen.

I wave. "Hey, Alex."

"Hey, Ellie." The other guy waits for Alex to say something, but when Alex doesn't speak up, he finally says, "Are you the girl living at the Martinson farmhouse?"

I tread water. Oh God, what does he know about my family? What has he heard about me? My throat tightens. I blink and force myself to stop worrying. "I'm Ellie. And

yes, I'm staying with my aunt and uncle for the summer."
I turn to Alex, hoping he'll give an introduction.

"This is Jake," Alex says with a slight nod.

Jake has big almond eyes, dark brown hair, broad shoulders, and a smile that makes me think he's actually happy. No wonder Amy thinks he's good-looking.

"And how do you know Alex?" Jake asks.

Alex splashes water in his face. "I told you. I do landscaping for her uncle." He turns to me. "Jake has a hard time believing I'm a landscaper."

I bite my lip to hide my smile. Then I dive and swim underwater, trying to get away from them. I pop up scouring the grassy area for Amy, who is now sitting on her towel paging through a magazine. I'm surprised she isn't jumping in the water, trying to talk to Jake. She seems more engrossed in letting her skin glisten in the sun.

Alex and Jake swim over again.

Alex reaches me first. "Hey, Ellie, want to go over to the rope swing?"

My choices are slim. I did not come to watch Amy suntan all day, especially since she's the one who wanted to hang out, so I agree.

Their faces get all excited, and Jake says, "Really? None of the girls ever go off the rope swing."

I raise an eyebrow. I'm not from this island, so I have no idea how I'm supposed to act. We scramble out of the water. Amy's lying on her stomach. She sits up when she sees Alex and Jake.

"I'm going to the rope swing," I tell her. "I'll be back in a little while, unless you want to come?"

"I'll swim after you get back," she says and barely opens her eyes. "Hi Alex," she says. Then, she lifts her head and smiles at Jake. "Hey, Jake. How's it going?"

He shifts his stance, swallows slowly, his eyes moving down every part of her. "I'm good," he says with an effort.

She flips the page of her magazine. "Maybe we can hang out later?"

"Sure."

Alex motions to Will. "Hey, Will, we're taking the new girl on the rope swing. Wanna come?"

I flinch when he calls me the *new girl*. I don't belong here. At all. And as if someone turned on a faucet, I'm overflowing with thoughts of how much I don't belong here. I start to see my mom, our trailer, even Jose, but force those thoughts back into to their cave with all the mental power I possess. I can't think about that.

Will touches Nadine's back, gentle like, and then gets up. "Sure, wait up."

Alex puts his arm on my shoulder and leads us to the path.

"Nadine, we'll try and bring him back alive," Jake yells as we climb the hill.

We run up the edge of the bank for about a hundred feet and head through a grove of pine trees. A huge branch hangs out over the edge of the cliff, dangling into the still water. The thought of flying through the air gives me a rush.

"OK, Ellie," Jake says. "I'll go first, and you can watch."

I stare at him for a second and then grab the rope. I can't handle the anticipation. If I don't go right this second, I won't go at all. I pull back and jump onto the rope, letting it swing me over the lake. When I'm as high as I can get, I let go and drop like a parachuter from an airplane, except without a parachute. I splash into the water. When I come up, all three guys are hanging over the edge.

Jake yells, "Are you all right, Ellie?"

I rub my eyes, "That was really fun."

"Well, aren't you full of surprises?" Jake grabs the rope. He steps even farther back than I did, does a body contortion in the air, and whoops loudly. Then he cannonballs into the lake.

Will jumps last.

When we're all treading water, I ask, "Are we going

again or what?"

Alex pushes my head under water. "Yeah, let's go."

We swim back to the edge, climb the hill, and pass the girls sunbathing.

"Maybe I can get Amy to come with us," I suggest.

"Good luck with that," Jake says. "Amy hardly ever gets in the water. She's too busy sunbathing and looking beautiful."

"Don't tell me you're complaining." Will pushes Jacob slightly.

"I'm not. She looks amazing – as always."

"I can at least try." I run over to Amy, who's still engrossed in her magazine. "Hey, Amy," I yell. "I just went off the rope swing. Are you sure you don't want to try it?"

"No way," she says.

"Come on, Amy, you should have seen Ellie." Jake calls. "She just grabbed the rope and flew into the air."

"Good for her, but I'm not jumping. I don't do heights," Amy says all cool like.

But I realize what the deal is: she's totally freaked out and doesn't want anyone to know, not to mention she's probably afraid that her perfect body won't look so perfect anymore. Please. She looks like she hasn't enjoyed a good meal in months. Not that I have either, but not for the same reasons.

"That's OK," I tell her. "Just watch us jump."

"All right." She shoves her magazine back inside her bag and stands, pulling Nadine with her.

She grabs her swimsuit cover up and wraps it around herself. *Yep.*

As we're going back to the rope swing, Nadine turns to me. "I'm Nadine," she says like I didn't just meet her about an hour before. "I'm sort of Will's girlfriend. He's Amy's brother."

"I'm Ellie," I say. Was she that oblivious to the fact that we just met, or is she making sure I know who's who on Orcas Island? She's worse than Amy. "Are you going to watch, or are you going to jump?"

She moves a few strands of hair out of her face. "If you can do it, I can do it."

A few minutes later, when she jumps, she lets out a bloodcurdling scream.

When we get tired and hungry, we walk back to town for lunch. Alex walks with me the whole way making funny faces. I shake my head at his bad jokes. Nadine and Will hold hands, and Jake and Amy pair off.

We select sandwiches at the café, and while Amy's wrapping them up, she suggests I stay at her house until the fireworks show.

I'm not sure I want to hang out much longer. "I have to change clothes and everything." I clutch my swim bag.

"You could just change upstairs in the loft, and then we won't have any trouble meeting up later. It gets crowded, Ellie."

The thought of a large crowd makes my stomach squirm, but I don't want them to know I'm a basket case. I've got to pull myself together.

*U*pstairs, their loft apartment is filled with farmhouse antiques, giving it warmth despite its small size. The kitchen table is piled with papers and bills, and the sink is overflowing with dishes. A black-and-white portrait of kids playing at the beach hangs over the mantel above the fireplace.

Nadine and I follow Amy into her room to kill some time before we head to the ferry dock.

Nadine stretches out on Amy's bed. "I'm exhausted." She closes her eyes and lets out a deep sigh. "I don't know how I'm going to stay up for the fireworks."

"You'll be fine," Amy mutters. "Besides, I'm sure my brother will keep you awake."

"Yes, he will." Nadine opens her eyes. "He's acting strange, though. He's even more quiet than normal, and that's saying something."

"Will and Nadine were a couple last summer," Amy explains to me, "and they sort of hooked up again the other night." She scrolls through the songs on her playlist.

"Geez, Amy, why don't you post it on Facebook too?" Nadine rolls onto her side and hugs one of the throw pillows.

I don't want to hear about Nadine and Will's drama. I get the feeling she's one of those superficial girls who just wants a guy to make herself feel important, but I'm not sure. I have other things to worry about.

Amy crinkles up her face. "I didn't know it was a secret." Her voice is laced with sarcasm.

Nadine's voice has an airy, daydreaming tone. "Hopefully, it'll turn into something more serious this summer," she says to me. "I don't just 'hook up' with anyone. I'm not that kind of girl. But with Will, it's special."

"I hope it works out for you guys," I say.

Nadine props up her head with a hand. "What about you, Ellie? Do you have a boyfriend?"

My stomach flips over. *I don't want to share anything with this girl.* "No. I kind of steer clear of relationships. I need to focus on school and getting into college and everything."

Jose is the closest thing I've ever had to a boyfriend, and it didn't really work. I thought I was in love with him and all that, but the only time we ever kissed, it was like kissing a relative. It weirded me out so much, I ended it.

Amy's eyes light up, and her voice gets this hopeful sound to it. "Alex seems pretty interested in you. You don't have to study during the summer, do you? It'd be fun for us all to hang out as couples."

I frown. "Alex is nice, but we hardly know each other."

I rummage through my bag and find I haven't brought a jacket with me. "Amy, can I borrow a sweatshirt or something? I forgot mine, and it'll cool down tonight."

"No problem. I just did a load of wash. I'll grab one out of the dryer."

She comes back with a Western Washington University sweatshirt.

I point to the logo on it. "Is this where you want to go?"

She's gathering blankets for the fireworks, but lifts her head. "No way," she says. "I'm going to beauty school to be a hairdresser. My dad wants Will to to play on the UW soccer team, but now all of a sudden Will wants to go to Western. One more thing for them to fight about."

"Where do you think he'll end up?" I'd love to go to Western but haven't figured out how to pay for it.

"Who knows, but right now it's all up in the air . My mom's so worried about him, she wonders if he'll make it through this year alive."

Nadine tucks her hair behind her ear. "He's fine. I don't know what the big deal is. He got kicked out of school, but he's smart and is still getting good grades and all."

Amy raises one eyebrow like Nadine is crazy. "Will is not fine. He got kicked out of two schools, quit the soccer team, and now he's going to parties in some very questionable places in Seattle and taking stupid risks no one should take, and the only time he talks to my dad is when they're fighting. He's a freaking train wreck, Nadine. You just hook up with him. I have to live with him."

Nadine's quiet for a second. "He needs a girlfriend. It's as simple as that. Once we're officially together, he'll calm down. Girls have a way of calming their guys down."

Amy holds out her hands like she wants Nadine to stop talking. "I'm not sure anything's going to calm Will down. But spare me the details. I'm sick of all the attention he gets."

Nadine stays quiet. I wonder how her plan is going to work. Will seems almost more disconnected from his life than I am from mine.

I break the silence. "So what year are you in school?"

"Amy and I are both going to be juniors. And you?"

"Senior." I grab my bag from the floor. "But I'm a year younger than most of the kids."

"Why?" Nadine asks. "Did you skip or something?"

"I was in a split class in elementary school. I worked up, and the teacher moved me up when I was in the third grade." I glance at the floor. I don't like talking about it. One more way I'm different than everybody else.

Amy's phone beeps. She picks it up, reads the message, and beckons us. "We need to go. Jacob just texted that we're going in Will's car. Not really enough room, but Alex or Jacob can jump in the back."

It's cooler outside, there's a slight evening breeze and Main Street is overflowing with people. Will drives up in a silver Subaru Outback, almost brand new. I can't believe it. I close my eyes and cringe inside. Why does it have to be an Outback?

Jacob and Alex jump out and help us into the car.

My stomach churns as we climb into the car. I try to ignore the flood of feelings, but it's hard. My palms dampen, my stomach swirls. I force myself to take a couple deep breaths. Memories stream back. I try to shove them aside like I did at the lake, but images keep showing up in my mind. The drug dealer on my porch steps, his face ugly, telling me he'll kill my mom, and me handing him my money. Then Jose's face when I told him I wasn't going to get the car. How he punched the trailer wall. My mom's face. *Oh, God, I have to get out of the car.* My stomach is sick, and my palms are sticky. I roll the window down and try to focus on what's outside.

I fiddle with my rings, trying not to get sick.

Amy taps me on the shoulder. "Put the window up, Ellie. Will has the air-conditioning on."

I hardly glance her way. I'm about to have a full on get-me-the-heck-out-of-here experience, and cute little

Amy doesn't even notice. My hands are trembling. I can't get enough air into my lungs. I'm shaking too hard to roll up the window.

"Amy, who cares about the window?" Will says. "If your friend wants it down, it's not a big deal."

What a relief. Thank you.

His tone and the way he distracted her gives me a moment to pull myself together. I close my eyes, let the fresh air rush past me, and force myself back to Orcas Island.

A little while later, I glance up at Will, hoping to thank him with my eyes. Nadine's sitting beside him, and they're holding hands. Before I have a chance to catch his eye in the rearview mirror, Nadine smiles at him with an I-want-you smile. He grips her hand and then glances at me in the mirror. I smile and give a half nod. I hope he sees I'm thankful.

My cheeks heat, and I avert my gaze. He glances out the window for a second and then removes his hand from Nadine's to take a sharp turn. He doesn't reach for her hand again. She snuggles closer, but he seems remote all of a sudden, like his mind is elsewhere.

He parks the car a few blocks from the ferry dock, and we all climb out. I'm more quiet than normal, still trying to hold onto my composure. Everyone seems engrossed in other things, so I doubt anyone notices. I set my bag on the grass a few feet away from the car and kneel over it, rearranging my stuff in a fragile attempt to gather myself together. I'm in a tug-of-war to keep my emotions under control, but they're dogged little suckers and won't let up.

I'm smoothing out my hair and taking deep breaths when I realize Will's focusing all his attention on me. He doesn't have that normal edgy look in his eyes. His eyes aren't defiant. His face is kinder, as if he's trying to convey that it's going to be all right.

It works. I get up and sling my bag over my shoulders. This guy is not acting the way I expected him to act. At all.

A while later, our blankets are spread on a big grassy hill overlooking the ferry dock, and I'm breathing freely and normally again. Somehow I ended up between Alex and Will. I don't want to sit too close to Alex, for fear he'll think I like him, and I don't want to sit too close to Will. He's unnerving. He's too aware of everything going on around him. His perceptive gaze makes me feel like it'd be easy to spill my guts to him. And I'm not going to do that.

Alex is chatting with Amy and Jake. Nadine walks over to talk to Amy.

Will flips onto his side so he's facing me. "I get the impression you don't like my car?"

I give a forced laugh. I don't want to talk about his car. "You noticed?"

He chuckles. "You are direct, aren't you?"

And you're unnerving. "Yes, I'm known for being direct. Anything wrong with that?"

He shakes his head. "No, but it could be a little intimidating to a more insecure guy."

I laugh. "Not you, of course." I reach into my bag and grab the sweatshirt that Amy handed me earlier. It's getting colder, so I slip it over my head.

Will points to the emblem. "Hey, are you going to Western?"

"In my dreams," I say. I rephrase my words. "I mean, it's where I'd really like to go next year. We'll see."

"So you're going to be a senior?" he asks, a hint of surprise in his voice. "Nadine said you were."

He probably thought I was younger. "Yep."

"Me too. Maybe I'll see you up at Western. I'll be there too."

"It's a big campus." I'm trying to act indifferent, staring down at the blanket, but this guy is intriguing.

He shrugs and opens a hand, palm out. His eyes light up in a playful manner. "You never know. So... what's at Western?"

"There's a program I want to get into."

He sits up with a genuinely interested look on his face. "Which one?"

His interest draws me deeper into the conversation, and I find I actually like talking to him. "Environmental science." My voice is cautious. I'm not convinced I want to tell him this.

"I didn't see that one coming."

"And you?" I shouldn't let him be the only one asking questions.

"I'm thinking history or English."

I nod. I almost ask him something about his reading, but then I stop. I'm not going to get interested in this guy. No matter what. I force myself to turn and see what the group is doing. They're having a grand time hanging out. Probably don't even remember I'm here. What a relief. Amy's laughing and has her arm on Jacob's leg.

"So what's your favorite book?" Will asks.

Before I can answer him, Jacob turns to us. "Hey, Ellie?" he asks. I scoot around on the blanket so I can see him. I guess they haven't forgotten that I'm here.

"How come you're staying with your aunt and uncle?" he asks.

His question surprises me. I manage to stutter, "They invited me is all." I grip my knees and lower my head, letting my hair shield my face. It's hard to swallow.

"Did your parents go on a trip or something?" Nadine scoots closer.

I don't know how to answer. "Yeah, something like that." My cheeks burn. My stomach tightens, and my eyes fill with tears. I finally say, "Um... I'm going to buy some popcorn." I grab my bag and force myself to my feet. I want to break into a run, to keep running and never come back, but I make myself stroll casually past the blankets.

As soon as I'm out of view, I dash away, wishing I hadn't come tonight. I don't know how to tell people she's gone. I haven't even told myself. And my dad? I don't even know his name.

I clench my fists. I don't want to cry.

I miss my mom. I miss having a mom. Before, people would ask me where my mom was and I'd say, "She works nights." She did. It wasn't a lie. Even though it was mortifying that my mom was a bartender and I lived in a trailer park, at least I had something to say. It doesn't matter if people ask questions when you have a good answer, but I don't have a good answer. My mom is dead, and it's my fault. I can't tell them the truth.

It takes a walk and the cool evening breeze to calm me. The roller coaster of emotions is wearing on me. I have to pull it together. After getting a bag of kettle corn, I wander through the crowd of people, trying to figure out how to go back to the group. After shoving half the bag of food down my throat, I make my way back. It's now dusk, and people are searching for their spots because the fireworks are about to begin.

When I return, Will sees me first and scoots over on the blanket to make room. Nadine's on the edge now, next to him. She has her arm through his. I sit beside him. Alex is texting someone on his phone, but he winks at me. *What's up with that?* Amy doesn't even notice I'm back. She's too busy talking to Jacob. Which is fine. I don't want any more attention.

Alex whispers, "I told everyone you were here to help take care of the kids this summer. That your Aunt Violet needed a break."

"Thanks, Alex." I tuck my hair behind my ears, but wonder how much he knows about what happened.

"I also told them to leave you alone. Enough with the questions already." His eyes widen, and he winks at me again.

I can't help but chuckle. I offer him some kettle corn. Alex is as innocent as a puppy. He's sort of annoying, but he means well.

"Don't worry about me," I say. "I'll be fine."

Nadine peeks around Will's chest. "Listen, Ellie. I'm

really sorry. Amy told us about your mom. Did she have cancer or something?"

My mouth drops open. *Oh my God. I want to fall into a hole. Everyone knows.* Before I can say a word, Will touches Nadine's side and moves in front of her.

"That's none of our business, Nadine." He looks right at me, his eyes big and clear. "May I have some kettle corn?"

I hold out the bag. "Sure."

Thankfully, the drama winds down because the fire-works begin. I lie back, using my bag as a pillow, and disappear into the bright lights flashing and falling overhead. Under the booms of exploding fireworks, I stop thinking and get swept up in the show. It calms me, quiets my inner chaos in a way that silence fails to do.

Then something weird happens with Will. My hands are at my sides, but Will's hand grazes the back of mine. He squeezes my hand, quick like, and lets go. I don't turn to him because I'm embarrassed. My face heats up. And despite how hard I'm fighting it, the way his hand, strong and fierce, gripped mine, part of me wants him to do it again.

After the grand finale, as the crowd is breaking up, a small girl stands crying on the side of the road. Her dark hair is tousled. The dust on her face has become dark streaks of mud down her cheeks. She's holding a big bag of popcorn, and her eyes are terrified as she frantically searches the faces around her. She's lost her parents.

I run over, kneel down in the dirt, and gently grip her shoulders. "What's your name?" I ask.

She only stares back.

I try speaking in Spanish.

She calms down when she hears her own language and tells me her name is Gabriela. Amy and the others gather around.

I wipe her eyes and hug her. "Where was the last place you saw them?"

She doesn't remember, but she tells me their names are Maria Jesus and Ignacio Fuentes. "I'm Ellie, and we're going to look for your parents." I stand up and tell her everything's going to be fine. She nods and stays close to me, sniffling every few seconds.

I tell everyone to look for Maria Jose and Ignacio Fuentes. Amy and Jacob take off together. Alex stays next to me. Will and Nadine go in the other direction. A few minutes later, Amy and Jacob come around the corner. A man with a worried look on his face is following them.

Gabriela sees him, and her eyes light up. "Papá," she cries.

She runs off, and her dad calls after me from a distance, "Gracias, gracias."

I wave, so relieved we've found her dad. At least one little girl found her family and gets to feel safe and secure tonight.

Hours later, when it's nearing midnight, we finally get back to the car. I'm exhausted and ready to be alone. It's tiring to be with people who have known each other their whole lives. I don't understand all the hidden meanings in everything they mention.

The crowds outside dwindle, but after we pile into the Subaru, we have to wait in the long line of exiting cars. I'm tired and not ready for the emotional roller coaster my stomach is threatening. I distract myself by counting stars on the way home, letting the conversation drift around me.

Will parks behind the café. Alex is spending the night at Jacob's house. Nadine lingers next to Will, but finally says goodnight. She goes in for a kiss, which I take as my cue to leave. I turn my head. Amy forgets about me while she says goodnight to Jacob. Then Jacob and Alex walk off with Nadine. She only lives a few houses down. I'm surprised Will isn't walking her home.

It's late. I say good-bye and start for the street.

"Ellie," Will calls after me, "I can drive you back."

I shake my head. "That's all right. I'll just walk." I don't want to get back in that Subaru.

Amy speaks up. "Ellie, it'll take Will five minutes to drive you home."

"I'll be fine. I'm going to walk."

"Why?" She rubs her eyes and yawns. "It's really late. Just let him take you home."

I swallow. "Fine."

I say good-bye to Amy and wait for Will to bring the car around.

Once I'm in the car, Will starts talking right away. It's like he's been waiting for the chance all night. "Your Spanish is good." He looks at me. "You didn't learn that in school."

"How do you know?"

"I've taken three years of honors Spanish, and I could never talk like you did."

Of course he'd notice. He notices everything. I take a deep breath and decide to tell him the truth. "I grew up in a trailer park on the outskirts of Seattle. It's like crossing the border to Mexico. Spanish was practically my first language."

"Oh." He sounds surprised. "So you live near Seattle?"

"Yeah."

"Cool," he says.

He's probably never set foot in a trailer park.

"And your issue with my car? What's that about?"

After clearing my throat, I turn the questions back over to him. "Since when did we decide to play twenty questions?"

He laughs. It's late, and his voice is low. My stomach flips over, and I squeeze my hand, remembering what it felt like when he clasped it so unexpectedly.

"Sorry. I noticed you got pretty upset when I drove

74

up. I couldn't figure out what was wrong until just now, when you didn't want to get in the car again."

"Maybe I'm just trying to keep my distance." I try to sound light and teasing, but I think he can see through me.

"I considered that." He grips the steering wheel and turns into my aunt's driveway. He slows the car down. "Listen, I'm sorry I was rude to you yesterday. I was in a bad mood. I shouldn't have said anything about the wagon. And then in the bookstore I was trying to be funny, but I probably came across like a jerk."

I'm not sure what to say. "Thanks." As he comes to a stop, I take my bag and open the car door.

"It wasn't me, though, was it?" he asks. "It has something to do with the car, right?"

I close my eyes for a second and take a deep breath. "I don't really want to talk about it, but no, it's not you. It's something else. Thanks for the ride."

He reaches over as I'm stepping out and holds out a hand. "Do you want to do something tomorrow?"

With one foot out of the car, I turn back toward him. "I don't think that's a good idea."

"The thing you said to my sister – about how you'd rather read the book than watch the movie – were you being serious?"

I'm getting really confused about why he wants to keep talking. "Yes. I like to read. It was sort of a key element in my survival. And most of the time I'd rather read the book than watch the movie." I step out of the car, but hold onto the door for a moment before closing it. "Listen, thanks for the ride."

"Bye, Eleanor," he says. "I'll see you around."

His eyes are warm, and I can't help but smile at him.

one day after the fireworks

The distance between the farmhouse and the lighthouse is about half a mile, all of which is on Violet's land. And the path from the lighthouse to the town is about three quarters of a mile. It's like a triangle. Seriously, who would have thought when living in my itty-bitty trailer that my mother was from a fifty-acre farm?

While I'm walking down the path the next day, I wonder how I can win the dog's trust. My strongest bet is through food and kindness. She'll accept me if I'm patient enough. But I hope that weird man doesn't show up again.

I take a cup of dog food and descend the narrow, steep trail. After I refill the dog's bowl. I sit there for a while, but when she doesn't come out, I return to the lighthouse, the long grass tickling my bare legs.

Will's the last person I ever expected to see here. He's on the path from my aunt's house, walking like he owns the trail.

He's holding a thermos and a small white paper bag. "I stopped by your house, and your aunt told me where I could find you." He steps closer and peers over the edge. "What were you doing down there?"

"Trying to help a dog." I can't figure out why he's here.

"Is the dog all right?"

"I think she's a stray. She won't let me come near her. I left her some food though." I glance back at him and then point to his hands, raising an eyebrow.

He answers before I have the chance to ask. "I brought some coffee and chocolate croissants from the café. Do you want some?" He lifts the bag and a stainless steel thermos.

I should have told Violet not to tell anyone where I was going, but it's not like I was expecting Will to come walking down the trail.

"Does anyone else know you're here?" I ask. "I wanted to keep this place a secret."

"I didn't tell anyone I was coming." He holds out the thermos again. "Do you want some?"

I shrug. "Sure. Thanks."

He fills the lid of the thermos and hands it to me. I take a sip, and it's rich with cream and sugar.

"So what brings you here?" I ask.

He glances down before he meets my stare. "Remember last night I asked if we could get together today?" He gestures toward the lighthouse. "Is this why you bought a book on lighthouses?" He focuses on the cottage for a moment. "That's a great lighthouse." Then he turns to me. "And the dog book...did you find one?"

I shake my head. "No. How do you know about that?"

"You asked the lady in the bookstore about books on lighthouses and dogs, remember?"

"I didn't know you were listening."

"It's a small bookstore." He points toward the door. "Do you have a key?"

"Why?" I shoot him a look like I think he's weird. Cuter than heck, but still weird. I don't get why he's trying to hang out with me, especially when he has a girlfriend.

He smiles. "I'd really like to see inside."

I shake my head like there's no chance this side of the water he's getting inside my lighthouse.

"How come?"

I bite the inside of my lip. "I don't want to show anyone right now. And I hardly know you. Besides, you'll probably tell your girlfriend." I shake my hand in the air, and my bracelets jangle. "No, not gonna happen."

His eyes widen. "Who said she's my girlfriend?"

"She did. Or at least she's pretty sure you're getting back together." I stare at the cliff trying to act as disinterested as possible.

"It's complicated with Nadine. We have a long...."

I cut him off. "I'm not really interested in hearing about your relationship. I just don't want her—or anyone else—to find out about this place."

"I wouldn't do that. I promise. But I'd really like to see inside." He holds out the white paper bag. "Besides we still have to eat the croissants.

I don't like where this is headed. I wanted to keep this lighthouse private. My mom came here. I'd hoped this would be a refuge. A place where I could escape and be alone. The last thing I want is visitors. If Will lets it slip, everyone will want to come by and check it out.

But I don't see any way to get out of showing him the lighthouse without being outright rude. I sigh internally. "I'll let you inside, but you have to promise you'll keep it a secret."

"Are we sharing secrets now?" His mischievous grin makes me laugh.

I hold his gaze for a moment, but then turn away, self-conscious. I open the front door. He follows me.

Once inside, Will takes a deep breath. "This is amazing."

After a few minutes, we climb the stairs and go outside. He sets his hands on the railing and stares off toward the sea as if he's thinking of something.

"It's incredible, isn't it?" I also rest my hands on the railing and gaze out across water. "In the afternoon, when there's no fog, you can see forever."

He turns around, his back against the railing. "Yeah, there's something to this place isn't there? Like a mystery or something. Imagine what it would be like restored."

"I'm planning to fix it up."

We stand in silence for a moment, and then to my surprise, he says, "Maybe I could help you?"

I keep my eyes on the view, at the play of sunlight on the water, pondering my response. I finally blurt out, "I don't get this. I'm confused about why you're here. You don't even know me."

He meets my gaze, as direct as anyone ever has. "I was sort of hoping to remedy that." He grips the railing with one hand and smoothes down his hair with the other. Then he licks his lips as if he's nervous. "Look, I know I was rude the first day we met, and you're becoming friends with my sister, but I liked talking to you last night. You're different than most people I know. I'd like to help you fix this place up...if you'll let me."

I swallow, trying not to be offended at how I'm "different from most people." I'm also thinking this could get messy. But something about his honesty throws me off guard. I believe him. I take a deep breath. "OK... But remember—"

He waves his hand in the air. "I know. I promise, I won't tell anyone. It'll be our secret."

"Not even your sister."

"Of course not."

"And not...Nadine."

He swallows. "Right."

And then I feel guilty. Nadine's his girlfriend or something close to it. He can't hide this from her. That's wrong. I sigh. "This isn't a good idea. You better not come again. I don't want you to have problems with your girlfriend, and I'm not into drama."

He drops his gaze and stares at his hands for a moment, his shoulders sagging a bit. "Look, Eleanor, I'm not into drama either. Nadine's got her own life. I'd like to have a friend who enjoys talking about books and stuff. Besides, this place is a mess. You could use the help."

I cross my arms and squint, thinking. Something about him intrigues me. He obviously loves to read, and he showed up here with a thermos of coffee. Not everybody would do that. "I'm not sure. I barely know you."

Will makes a pleading look with his eyes. "I'd really like to help you with this. It's a cool lighthouse. I'm a nice guy. I know I acted like a jerk the other day at the café, but that's not normally how I am."

I eye him up and down. "I guess... I could use the help."

I hold out my hand to shake, and he wraps his hand around mine. There's a funny flip inside me, and my breath stops for a moment. I pull my hand away, and we head back down into the cottage.

For the rest of the afternoon, we discuss all the different ideas for the lighthouse. How to repair the light to make it functioning. Whether I should paint the outside or not. If it's possible to revive the roses that are overgrown and dormant. The more we talk, the more I find I enjoy his company. I like that he accepts who I am without asking a lot of questions.

After we're done planning, I ask what everyone said last night when I went to buy popcorn.

He shrugs. "Do you really care what they said?"

My back's against a wall, my knees are tucked up, and I stare at the ground. "I guess not. I mean, I hardly know them, but I feel bad. They weren't trying to be rude."

"It's your life, Ellie. You don't have to tell anybody anything unless you want to."

"That's true, I guess."

Before we head out in different directions, we decide when to meet the following day after he's done his shift at the café. He agrees to bring sponges and window cleaner. I'll bring buckets, soap, and dust rags.

"So tomorrow afternoon?" I ask as I lock the door to the lighthouse.

"Sounds good." I turn to walk back to Violet's, but he just stands there.

"What's wrong?"

"My car's at your aunt's house. Can I walk with you?"

"Oh, right."

As we walk back to the house, my stomach flips all around again. I catch him looking at me out of the corner of my eye from time to time and wonder what he's thinking.

He finally says, "You never told me what your favorite book is."

I grin. "That's true. It's *Jane Eyre*. And yours?"

"*The Lord of the Rings*. I've read the trilogy like four times."

"I read them the first time when I was thirteen. Then again last year. Definitely top ten."

"They're great, but I'm trying to figure out why *Jane Eyre* is your favorite book?"

I run my hand over my hair. Self-conscious. "I like her resilience. She survives without letting it make her hate, and in the end she finds happiness." I turn to him. "And why is *Lord of the Rings* your favorite?"

"For lots of reasons, I guess. Maybe for how hard they fight against evil."

When we get to the driveway, we stop in front of his Subaru. Once again, I stiffen, and my stomach turns to knots. Every muscle in my face tightens.

Will sets his hand on my arm. "Are you going to tell me about the car? Why it bothers you so much?"

I bite my lip and force my fear and discomfort to retreat into the corners of my mind. "Probably not."

"Just so you know, I wouldn't say anything to anyone else."

I raise my eyebrows and force a half grin. "Thanks for

as waters gone by

the coffee. I need to get inside."

"So tomorrow, right?" he asks.

"Tomorrow."

I climb up the porch steps.

Inside, Violet's sitting at her desk going over some papers. She lifts her head. "Did Will find you?" I can tell she's trying hard to hide her interest.

"Yeah."

"And...?"

Before she says anything else, I interrupt her. My voice sounds lighthearted, surprising me. "He's nice. Likes to read books."

"Are we going to be seeing more of Will around here?"

I clear my throat. It's weird she asked me that. My mom never cared about my life. At all. "He's got a girlfriend, so I highly doubt it." I pull out my phone and head toward the kitchen. "I'm going to call Jose."

Violet goes back to her paperwork with a slight grin on her face.

A loaf of fresh bread is cooling on the counter. The smell distracts me. After I cut a slice and smother it with butter and fresh strawberry jam, I call Jose.

He answers on the first ring. "I was just going to call you," he says. "You're doing better, aren't you?"

"How'd you know?"

"Hard to explain. I just do."

I clear my throat. "There's this old lighthouse I found the other day. Rundown and sad-looking. I think I'm going to fix it up."

"That's great, Ellie. How was the Fourth? Did you do anything fun?"

"I went to the fireworks with some kids from around here."

"And... how are you?" Jose's tone indicates he means on a deeper level.

"I miss you like crazy, but I'm all right. Still here."

"I miss you too." His voice cracks, and I know he

misses me so much it hurts.

We talk about the lighthouse, the cousins, Violet and Ben, and Amy, but I don't tell him about Will. I'm not sure why, but I don't.

Later that night I sit in the window seat, gazing out at the night sky. I can't stop thinking about Will. I can't believe he showed up with coffee and croissants. Completely random. Like cool random. He even wanted to know about *Jane Eyre*.

I've never met a guy who cares about what I'm reading. Jose knows I love books, but it's not like he asks me about them. There's something about Will Larson that I'm not sure what to do with. He's ruining my first impression of him. I thought he was a total player, and now I'm not sure I was right. It's like that's what he wants people to think about him, but there's something else there, underneath. He's definitely unique.

What will it be like working at the lighthouse together? My heart speeds up. It's the first time since I arrived on the island that I'm excited – and nervous – about the next day.

secrets told

The next afternoon Violet has laid out a huge sheet for the kids. The twins are sleeping in their swimming trunks, and Prissy's asleep in her bright pink swimsuit right next to them. I lie down close to Mikey, or at least I think it's him. His skin is hot and soft against me. His breathing, gentle and slow, falls into a quiet rhythm.

Back in Seattle, I always wished my family were bigger. I was jealous of how close the kids in the trailer park were to their brothers, sisters, and cousins. Everyone has someone, and they stick together no matter what. Lying next to my cousins warms me on the inside, and the loneliness that has plagued me ebbs for a moment.

Then guilt, like a hand constricting my heart, squeezes inside of me, making it hard to breathe. I almost get up and go into the house. But listening to my cousins' rhythmic breathing, I find myself matching their cadence, and my heart slows. I close my eyes and sleep.

Gabe wakes me up, by patting my cheek. He studies me as I open my eyes. "Ellie," he whispers. "Mommy says we have the same color eyes. She says that your eyes are sad, but they'll get happy again." His breath smells like peanut butter and jelly.

I sit up. "Do you think my eyes are sad?" I touch his bare arm.

His arms are a toasted golden color from the sun, and his eyes are dark brown like mine.

"Yep. But they're not gonna stay sad. Mommy says that your sad parts will blow away with the summer wind, and love will fill you up."

I choke. Can't breathe.

He gets so close our noses touch. "She says love just runs out the bottom of you right now." He motions with his hand flowing toward the ground. He pats my cheek with his small chubby hand. "Don't be sad, Ellie."

All I can see are his brown eyes. I blink fast, trying to get past the tears, and pull him into a tight hug. "Gabe, what am I going to do with you?"

Mikey wakes up and jumps into our hug. Then Prissy rouses and jumps on me too. Soon, we're tickling and wrestling on the ground, and as if from somewhere far away, I hear myself laugh. It catches me off guard. I hardly recognize the laughter. It's coming from deep inside.

I pause for a second. Guilt crouches around the laughter and tries to squelch it. But the kids tickle me some more, and I let myself go. I laugh, and the kids laugh with me. Their eyes sparkle, their mouths gape as their whole bodies shake. It's like cool water splashing through me.

Finally, I tell the kids I need to go. It's not right for me to be so happy, and Will will be waiting. I hurry to the garden. Aunt Violet's on her knees, pulling weeds. A round straw hat hides her face from the sun, and her bare hands are deep in the dirt. She never wears gardening gloves, so her hands always have remnants of dirt stained into the creases.

"Violet, I'm going to the lighthouse, unless you have

a job for me."

"Nope. You go have fun." She pats her hands, and dust billows off them. She stretches her back, bending and arching. "I heard you laughing with the kids just now."

"Yeah?" I shift back and forth.

She squints and stares for a minute. "It reminded me of your mom."

"It did?" My mom didn't laugh.

"Your mom had a laugh that made everyone around her want to laugh."

Oh. My throat constricts. I don't want to think there might have been a time when she was actually happy. I've always wondered if it was my fault she was sad. Knowing she was happy a long time ago makes the reality of it hit me.

"Thanks for telling me that, Violet." I mean it, but I've got to get out of there. I can't talk about who my mom was before she left this island. It's too much.

I escape to the lighthouse.

Before going inside, I climb down to check on the dog. Will's kneeling in the grass, directly in front of the dog's cave. He's silent and still. When I reach him, he takes my hand and pulls me down next to him. He smells fresh out of the shower, with that combination of soap and musky cologne. It makes me move closer. I can't focus.

"She had the babies, Ellie." His voice is low.

"Oh, my gosh," I whisper. My heart beats faster as I peek inside her cave. "How can you tell?" It's so dark, I can't see anything.

"Because she isn't moving. If you're quiet, you can hear them suckling."

I pause for a second, and sure enough, in the far reaches, I catch the faint sound of puppies suckling. They're probably adorable. "We should leave her extra food," I say, wishing I could see them. "I wonder how many pups she had?"

He gives me a very serious look. "Ellie, is that dog

wild?"

"I'm not sure. Something's wrong with her. She's scared of people."

"You have to be careful. She'll be worse with the pups."

"I don't want to hurt her, Will. I want to help her."

"That might not be possible."

"How would you know?"

He sits in the grass, pulls one of the blades, and runs it through his fingers. "We had a dog who went crazy from immunization shots. He was beyond help."

"Do you think that's what happened to this dog?"

"I don't know. But from the distance, she has the same wild-eyed look."

I turn away from him and stare back at the dog's cave. I don't argue with him, but I know I can help that dog. She needs consistency. "What should we name her?"

"Ellie, that dog is not a pet."

"I think we should call her Maggie. We can name the pups once we know how many there are." I stand, dust myself off. "Are you ready to work on the lighthouse?"

Will takes my hand as we climb the steep path. When we get to the top, he's still holding it, so I gently pull it away.

I take the key from the porch light and open the door. A blast of fiery hot air shoots out. It's way hotter than I can bear. "Whoa, maybe we should come back after it cools off?" he suggests.

"We could. Or maybe we should start coming early in the morning before it gets hot?" I like to get up early, and it would keep me from having to explain where I'm going. "We could meet before breakfast," I suggest.

"Sounds good to me." Will walks into the front room.

It's smoldering. Little beads of sweat drip down the side of my face.

Will starts opening windows. "Everyone's going to the stargazing hill tonight. Do you want to come?"

"I'm not sure. What's the stargazing hill?"

"Just this place where locals like to hang out. We hike up at dusk and watch the stars come out. It's cool."

"Maybe not. Especially if we'll be working on the lighthouse so early tomorrow morning." I'm not sure I'm up to being around a big group of people.

"It'll be fun. You should come."

We hang out on the balcony for a while, staring out at the sea. In the distance a ferry glides across the water, and a gentle breeze catches the trees, rustling their leaves. Other than that, it's silent, still. We don't talk. It's a peaceful silence. For a moment, the guilt claws inside me, trying to assault my heart, my mind. But sitting with Will, in his presence, it loses its power. I don't get it, except that Will seems at ease with himself, and it puts me at ease too.

Later, we walk through the cottage and close all the windows. When we step outside, the old man appears in the doorway. Our eyes lock. I freeze.

His mouth twists, and his eyes darken. He shakes his cane at us. "I told you to stay away from this place."

Tingles shoot down my spine.

Will steps closer to me, puts a hand on my shoulder, and shields me from the old man. "Who are you?"

The man sets his cane down, rests on it, and shakes his fist. "That don't matter," he shouts. "This is Rose's lighthouse. I'm watching it for her. For when she comes back."

I gasp. Stumble backwards a couple of steps. Will's hand tightens on my shoulder, keeping me from falling.

Why did that man say my mom's name? I tremble. I take deep breaths, but can't get enough air. Will takes my hand, and this time I don't pull it away. I grip it.

"We were just leaving," he tells the old man.

I lock the door with shaking fingers. It takes several tries. I don't put the key back in the porch light, but instead tuck it into my pocket.

Will gently guides me down to the path toward the beach. My hands are shaking. I can't talk. Can't breathe.

Can't see straight.

He wraps his arm around me for a moment to lower me onto a fallen log. I try to pull myself together, but I can't seem to stop shaking.

"It's OK, Eleanor. I think he's harmless."

I shake my head and try to explain. "It's not that. It's something he said."

Will settles beside me and gazes into my eyes, his hand still touching my arm. "What was it?"

I press my hands to my cheeks and whisper so quietly he has to bend closer to catch my words. "Rose was my mom's name."

"Oh, God."

I nod, wide-eyed.

"No wonder you got so freaked out." He clutches my hand.

It helps me focus.

"Do you think he was talking about her?"

"I don't know."

We sit in silence for a few minutes.

"What happened to your mom, Ellie?" Will's question comes out in such a caring way, it takes me off guard.

I stare at the sand. "What do you mean?"

He waits a few seconds. "I know she died. I'm really sorry. I was wondering what happened."

Oh, God. Not now. I can't do this now. I can't talk about this. The guilt, the accusation that it's all my fault weighs me down. The words are right there, but I can't make them come out of my mouth. I slowly pull my hand out of his and stand. I dust the sand off my shorts frantic like.

"She just died is all," I say. I turn to walk away, but I turn back around, daring myself to say something true. "But, if I could do one thing, just one – I'd go back to the day before she died, and I'd change things."

I walk away. Guilt hovers like fog, suffocating me. I have to get out of there. I don't want to be with Will anymore.

He asks too many questions at the right moment. Most people ask questions in the wrong moment, and they get tired of waiting for answers. Will doesn't. He's one of the only guys I've come across who balances asking the right question with knowing when to back off. It's unnerving.

I'm halfway up the path before I realize he's right behind me. I feel his presence, but I ignore him, hoping he'll leave me alone. Once I get to the top of the hill, I head for home.

Will meets my stride, walking beside me. He takes my hand again and squeezes it like he wants tell me something without words. I don't look at him. Instead, I stare at the dirt, but I leave my hand in his. He holds it all the whole way home. It isn't romantic. But it is tender.

"Would your aunt mind if I eat dinner at your house?" he asks when we get to the driveway, like he isn't ready to leave me. "I can walk you into town for the stargazing. You wouldn't have to go alone."

"I don't think I'm going stargazing," I tell him. "But I'll see if you can stay for dinner."

"Sounds perfect." He grins at me as if he has a secret.

"What?" I ask, curiosity getting the better of me.

"Nothing, Eleanor," he says under his breath. With his free hand, he lifts a strand of my hair and runs his finger down it.

I get goose bumps. He stares at me like he's studying everything about me, memorizing me, and I don't understand why.

I gulp under the scrutiny of his gaze and shift my weight. "Are you hungry?" I ask.

"Starving," he says, which breaks the intensity, and we laugh.

Something shifts inside me. It's like some of that fog has dispersed, making more room to breathe. Who knew that by telling someone she was gone, I'd feel better?

When we get to the house everyone greets Will, and Violet says he's welcome to stay for dinner. My aunt and uncle eye me, but they don't ask any questions.

While we eat, the kids ask him a million questions. They especially want to know about soccer.

Ben passes Will some mashed potatoes. "Are you going to school on the island this year?"

"I'd like to. That's what I'm trying to figure out with my parents right now."

Violet glances at him. "Would you play soccer for the school?"

He shakes his head, chewing on a bite of chicken. "I quit. I don't think I'll be kicking the ball around any time soon."

Violet sets her fork down. "I always enjoyed watching you play. You're good."

Will swirls some butter into his potatoes, and keeps stirring. "Thanks."

Prissy pours herself some juice. She smiles at Will about three times. I think the girl's crushing on him. "You should show Will your room, Ellie. It's the best room in the house. My dad worked on it for days before you got here."

"I'm sure he doesn't want to see my room, Prissy."

"Why not?" she says taking a sip of her juice. "It's got a window seat. Ellie sits there a lot."

My face heats up, and I swallow.

Will picks up his glass and pours himself a cup of milk. The whole table is silent, like no one's quite sure what to say.

Ben pushes back his chair and pats his stomach. "That was great, honey," he says to Violet. And then almost as an afterthought as he's picking up his plate, he says, "It is a great window seat, if I do say so myself."

Prissy gives me a smug smile. "I told you." She picks up her plate too and sets it in the sink.

I finish the last of my food and expect to walk Will to his car, but he says, "Aren't you going to show me your window seat?"

I frown. "No." I set my plate in the sink. "If I hardly wanted to show you the lighthouse, I'm definitely not going to show you my room. If you haven't figured it out by now, I'm kind of a private person."

"Ah, come on. Your cousin says it's great. I'd like to see it."

"Why?"

"Why not?" he says with a shrug and his cute smile.

"Because it's private. That's why."

"Oh, come on. I'm not going to tell anyone. I want to see the window seat."

"Fine."

We walk up the two flights of stairs. It's chilly inside my attic room because of the small air conditioner in the far window. Will studies everything. He glances at the very old quilt on my bed.

"Violet says it was my mom's," I tell him.

"That's cool." Will walks over to the nightstand and picks up a picture of me, Maria, and Jose laughing on the Ferris wheel at the Evergreen State Fair. "Who're they?"

How much I should say, particularly about Jose? "I grew up next door to them," I say. "I spent most of my time at their house."

"You look really happy in this picture."

"I was."

Will sets it down, walks to the window seat. He peeks through the window and sits down. I think he's about to say something when footsteps march up the stairs.

Prissy peeks in the doorway. "Mom wants to know if you guys want brownies for dessert?"

Will laughs. "I'm going to head out, but thanks. Oh, and Prissy?" he says.

She puts her hand on her hip. "Yeah?"

"It is a cool window seat."

"Told you," she says to me.

I walk Will down to the front door and say good-bye.

"Thanks, Eleanor."

"For what?"

"For telling me about your mom."

I swallow. I give him a slight smile as I study the cracks in between the wood on the front porch. He wouldn't say that if he knew the whole story.

"See you tomorrow morning?" he asks.

"Tomorrow."

Later when I'm lying in bed, memories of Will scroll through my mind. The way he fingered my hair. Even his shower-fresh smell lingers around me.

My thoughts drift to my mom. So much about her is like a blank sheet of paper – her life, her past. Who was she before she had me? That old man spoke her name like he knew her, but who was he, and what did he know?

the stargazing hill

We don't see the old man for more than a week. Ever since he said the lighthouse was Rose's lighthouse, I've got this urge to find out more about him or ask if he knew my mom, but it all makes me freeze up. I wish I had the courage to find out what happened to her. Even if her problems were because of me, I've got to know. My mom still flashes into my mind, and my chest gets tight, my stomach turns to knots, and I can't breathe. But now at least I can be with everyone without getting so paralyzed and freakish.

Thankfully, summer moves into a rhythm of its own. Will and I work in the lighthouse every morning. We wash the windows, dust, mop the floors, and cut the grass. Somehow he managed to get a ladder and the weed whacker from his mom's house. It's tricky getting all our supplies there without anyone knowing about it.

In the afternoons, I walk into town, grab something from Julie's Café, and either go shopping with Amy or head off to the lake. I usually offer to take the kids with me, but most of the time, Violet keeps them with her, and they hang out at the house. Sometimes Will's working at the café, but we both act like we hardly know each other.

It's weird keeping the lighthouse restoration, and my friendship with Will, a secret from the group. Even though I'm still reserved and haven't answered their questions about my mom or how she died, I'm more connected to everyone, and I'm beginning to feel less like a floating buoy. I feel heavier, like I'm not going to drift away anymore.

Other than the day I told Will about how I wish I could change things with my mom, we don't talk about personal stuff. We don't discuss Nadine, where things are at with them, how long I'm staying on the island. He doesn't ask about my mom, and I don't ask about his parents. There's a silent agreement between us that we work on the lighthouse – no questions asked. We don't have to prove anything or say more than we want to say.

Because of this, I'm really surprised when Will changes the rules. We're washing the outside of the cottage and disagreeing about painting it. I don't have the time or the money. Besides, I like the rustic look. We agree to wash the walls and see how it looks. Which isn't easy to do because paint chips peel off and fall in chunks to the ground.

"Ellie?"

I'm on a ladder, reaching as high as I can to clean. "Yeah?" I call down.

"Tell me about your life before you came to the island."

I squint and scrub harder. "What do you mean?"

"Tell me something, anything," he says. "Where'd you live? Your best friend? You know, stuff like that."

I pause, then step down a few rungs. Will reaches for my hand and helps me off the ladder, which gives me time to think.

We find a clean spot in the grassy area and sit. I tuck up my knees and rest my head on my legs. Part of me wants to tell him about my life. The other part's totally freaked out about what he'll think.

"I grew up in a trailer park in Bothell, near Seattle. My best friend is Jose Lopez. His mom used to take care of me after school." I turn toward him.

"Is he your boyfriend?" Will's voice has a tight edge to it.

I shake my head. "Naw, we're just friends. We thought about it, but he's more like a brother. I can't imagine it ever being romantic."

I change the subject. "I love science. I love the earth. I'd like to go to law school one day and eventually work in public policy. And you?"

"What about me?" he asks.

I point across the land. "Your life away from the beauty of this island?" I say. "You do have one right?"

"Not much of one. At least not anymore. I go to an all-boys private school." He rolls his eyes. "Sometimes parents just don't get it."

"True." I leave it there. "And your friends?" I raise my eyebrows again.

"Yeah, I have a few friends." He smirks, and I get the impression he probably has a lot of them.

Very different from me. I have a small circle of people I can trust, and after everything with my mom, that circle got even smaller. I need to call Jose and Maria soon. I'm sure they're worried about me.

"I had friends from my soccer team and stuff, but Alex and Jacob have been my best friends since we were kids. We used to play soccer together every summer, until I quit."

"You mentioned that at dinner the other day. What's the deal with you quitting?"

"Didn't want to do what my dad wanted me to do."

I'd like to ask him about his dad, but I'd better not push too hard. "Were you any good?"

"Used to be. Now I read books and restore antique lighthouses." He picks up a blade of grass and runs it through his fingers.

I chuckle. How good a soccer player was he?

"And your mom?

"What about her?" I tuck my hair behind my ears.

"What did she do for work?" His voice is quiet, thoughtful.

"Bartender at a tavern." I force my voice stay even.

"How old was she?"

I pinch my lips together to fight the well of emotion that threatens to tumble out of me. My shoulders tighten. If he wants to ask me about my mom, I'm going to ask about his family. "Are you going to tell me about you and your dad?"

"Why do you want to know about that?" he asks, rubbing his leg.

"I don't know. I guess I'd like to know what happened with your parents." I stare at him for a second. "Only if you want to tell me, I mean."

"My mom and dad got divorced a couple years ago."

I wait in silence, thinking he'll say more, but he doesn't. "Is that why you're so mad at him?"

Will stares off into the distance. "I don't know. The whole thing was crap." He throws the blade of grass onto the ground.

"Where is he now?" I ask.

"In Seattle, in the same house where we grew up."

"Did he get remarried or something?"

Will shifts around and takes a deep breath, twisting his hands. "Something like that. Geez, when did we start playing twenty questions?"

"I don't know. I was happy washing the walls."

"I don't like to talk about my dad. Nothing personal. I just don't want to talk about him. Ever."

Whoa. "That's fine. But here's the thing. Don't ask me a bunch of questions if you have no intention of answering any."

I stand and pick up the handle of a bucket full of water

to start back up the ladder, but then, on impulse, I put my hand in the water and fling soapy water at his back.

Will whirls, fire in his eyes. He takes the other bucket filled with dirty water, and throws twice as much at me. I scream. "You. Are. So. Going. To. Get. It."

I toss the entire bucket at his chest and drench his white shirt. He stands there like a wet dog, breathing deeply, and then he takes hold of my arm. I cry, laugh, and jerk, struggling to get away, but he dumps his bucket of much dirtier water over my head. I'm practically hysterical at this point, gripping his arm. I tumble onto the grass laughing, and because he's holding my arm, he falls on top of me. He's heavy, and wet, and... gorgeous.

We both stop laughing at exactly the same moment.

I swallow, staring into his eyes.

He props himself up just enough to take his full weight off me, but he stays where he is. When he brushes a few wet hairs off my face, I can't breathe. His chest rises and falls against my own. He rubs my cheek with his thumb, staring into my eyes. I don't know what to do. He cups my cheek and moves closer. He's going to kiss me. I want him to kiss me.

I startle, remembering Nadine. I can't do this. I muster my strength and turn my head to the side, twist out from under him, and stand, wiping the grass stains from my shorts.

"I have to go," I say. "I'll talk to you later."

I leave him sitting in the grass. My heart is racing. How could I have let that happen? He has a girlfriend.

Several hours later, I'm sitting on the front porch, trying to act like I didn't almost kiss Will, and fighting regret that we didn't kiss. What would it have been like to kiss him? For just a second, when he brushed the hair off my face, I let myself think that maybe something could happen between us.

More than likely he'll never try that again. Do I embarrass myself by having a talk, or do I assume he understands and just let it go? AAAHHH! Besides, at the end of the summer I'm going back to the trailer park, and I won't see Will again.

He texts while I'm sitting on the porch still trying to breathe.

Will: You OK?
Me: Fine.
Will: Want to talk later?
Me: Not really. Maybe you should go out with your girlfriend.

Right now I'm babysitting the kids. Violet needed to run some errands and get her hair cut. She gave me a few instructions, saying she'd be back in time for dinner, which Ben's bringing home. She hugs and kisses me on her way out. I pat her on the back a couple of times. I know she's trying to be nice and all, but there are moments when I'd like to beg her to stop slobbering over me. It's too much too soon.

Inside, Prissy is at the kitchen table coloring a bright picture of her family. She points everyone out to me. "Here's Goldie, Mikey, Gabe, Mommy, Daddy, and me. And here's you, Ellie." She put me between her and Violet. "I'm glad you came to live with us. I think you're pretty. You wanna color with me?"

"Sure." I try to keep my voice from cracking. I'm going to miss them when I leave at the end of the summer. "Why don't I draw a picture of the lighthouse I'm fixing? I'm going to take you there to show you when I'm all done."

She keeps coloring, but says with her head down,

"Mommy says your mom used to go to that lighthouse every day. She was waiting for someone, but he never came."

I gasp. Who was my mom waiting for?

A little while later, the kids and I make cookies – chocolate chip – and set them on a bright red tray. Each of us eats two, along with a tall glass of cold milk, and then we play in the grass.

Before I know it, Ben is driving up in his pickup. Behind him, in Will's silver Subaru, my new friends cruise down the driveway.

Will parks off to the side, and Amy, Alex, Jake, and Nadine jump out of the car. I stand at the kitchen door, sure my mouth is hanging open.

Alex sees me first. "Ellie, we were driving down the road to see you, and your uncle invited us all over for dinner."

I wave. "Good."

Ben calls out. "There's always room for friends."

Amy and Will are holding big bottles of soda. Alex and Jake hold up boxes of ice cream bars, and Nadine has bags of microwave popcorn.

Ben ruffles Will's hair on his way in. "Good to see you again, Will."

"Thanks, sir," he says.

Amy gives Will a funny stare, then glances at me. "See you again?" she asks.

Will ignores her. Our gazes meet, and I can't help but smile at him.

"What brings you all over to see me?" I ask as they file into the kitchen.

"We were worried when you didn't show up at the lake today," Amy says. "Even though it's kind of cloudy, you almost always come into town in the afternoon."

Jake pipes up, "Will suggested we come over to make sure you're all right." Jake furrows his brow. "Now why would Will suggest that?" he asks.

Nadine scoots over to Will and puts her hand through his arm. "Ellie's new in town. I'm sure Will just wants her to feel welcome."

"What're we going to do for dinner?" I ask Ben.

"I ordered pizza a few minutes ago when I ran into everyone on the road. Violet's going to pick it up. She'll be here in a few minutes."

"Guess it's all worked out." I say. "Can I get anyone something to drink?"

Alex nudges Amy. "You brought drinks. I'll have some of the cream soda."

My cousins start talking to everyone. Prissy tells Amy how pretty her hair is, and how she hopes when she's older, she'll have hair exactly like hers, which couldn't happen even if Prissy brushed her hair for two hours a day. The twins are talking to Will and Jake about their big trucks. Nadine is standing off to the side, her arms crossed. She sidles closer to Will, trying to show him something on her phone, but he's too busy with the twins. Alex is standing beside me, and he smiles whenever I notice him. He helps me set out napkins and plates after I get everyone something to drink.

Violet drives up a few minutes later, carrying an armload of pizza. She tells us all to wait for her outside, while she sets the pizza on the table. "I'll call you when everything's ready."

We step out onto the porch. I lean against the railing and sip my drink. Will comes up beside me and runs his hand over my arm, gentle like. Nadine's got her nose to her phone and doesn't see. He stands next to me for a minute, but Alex moves over to me, bumping him out of the way.

Alex nudges me. "Did Will tell you? We want to go to the stargazing hill tonight. It's supposed to clear up. There's a meteor shower."

I shake my head. "Nobody said anything to me."

Without looking at me, Will asks, "Do you want to

go?"

I sip my soda. "I don't know if my aunt and uncle want me out that late."

Alex pipes in, "Oh, don't worry about them. I talked to your uncle in town and promised to walk you home."

Amy glances up from the porch swing. She and Jake are sitting close to each other, talking in low voices. "So do you want to go, Ellie?" Her wide blue eyes sparkle.

"I guess so." I'm not convinced this is a good idea. I'm not sure how to act around Will, and Nadine's prancing around like she owns him. Alex won't stop looking at me, but he's the least of my worries.

I'm not sure what to do about Will. I don't know whether to talk to him about the almost kiss, or let it go. Maybe it's better to pretend it never happened. In reality, nothing happened. I feel a twinge of heartache, like maybe I'm losing something. But I shove it aside. It wasn't like he was ever mine to lose.

Violet calls us into the house. She and Ben sit at the kitchen table with the kids, so we can have the dining room. The guys consume a whole pizza in the time it takes me to eat one piece.

"Hey, Ellie," Alex says, "don't you live in the attic? Could we see it?"

"You want to see my room?" I take a bite of sausage pizza and inwardly cringe.

Amy wipes her hands on her napkin. "Only if you don't mind showing us."

I take a sip of soda, washing down my last bite of pizza. "I guess so."

We all troop up the stairs to the third floor. I'm glad I picked up my dirty laundry earlier today.

"So this is it." I say as everyone crowds into the room. Will stands off to one side and peruses my books. Jake and Amy sit on my bed and whisper to each other. Then Amy giggles under her breath and rests her head on Jake's shoulder. Nadine, who said about four words all through dinner, walks over and stands next to Will. She takes his fingers and works them into her hand. Alex sits in the window seat.

"I like your room, Ellie," Amy says.

"Thanks." I rest against the door frame. After a few minutes, Will who hasn't spoken or looked at me since we were on the porch before dinner, marches over to my door. "Are we going tonight or not? If we're not going, I think I'll go home."

Alex holds his hands up in the air like he's surrendering in a gun fight, "Wow, Will. You OK?" He stands. "All right then, let's go."

Everyone gets up. Nadine reaches for Will's hand again. He fidgets and shakes her hand off. All of us descend down the narrow, steep stairs.

Violet's in the kitchen cleaning up, while Ben watches a cartoon with the kids. He glances up at us. "You kids going to the stargazing hill?"

"Is that all right?" I ask. "I'm happy to stay and clean up. We're the ones who made the mess."

Violet yells from the kitchen. "You babysat all afternoon. I'm happy to clean up."

Ben's pulling Gabe's pajamas over his head. He looks up at me. "Alex said he'd walk you home. Isn't that right?" My uncle raises one eyebrow in Alex's direction and scans him over.

"Yes, sir." Alex answers as if he's talking to an army drill sergeant.

"I guess we can go then." I've never been to a stargazing hill before.

Everyone thanks my aunt and uncle for the pizza. I grab a coat and a few blankets to sit on, and then we drive to the trailhead in Will's car. I'm thankful I don't panic when we get in the car.

On the hike we walk in a large cluster. I attempt to dawdle behind, but Alex sticks close to me and barely gives me room to breathe. Will stays as far away from me as possible, and Nadine speaks in a quiet voice, so he has to bend close until they're only centimeters apart. My throat tightens. I try not to think mean thoughts about Nadine, but they're rolling in like thunderclouds. My heart is harboring conflicted emotions. I like that Will and I almost kissed. But I don't want to cause any problems with Nadine, and I'm leaving at the end of the summer.

Amy laughs at all Jake's jokes and walks as close to him as she can. Once in a while, when she thinks no one is looking, they hold hands.

We get to the top and spread out. Will sits next to Nadine like he's a part of the rock he's beside. Despite the fact that I'm seriously trying not to make Alex think I like him or anything, I don't move away when he first inches close to me. All I can think is *Please don't hold my hand. Oh, please don't hold my hand.* I press my hands tightly against my legs and scoot over a bit so he won't get any ideas.

Overhead, the stars are amazing. They shine brightly, illuminating the darkness and twinkling as if in a dream. The patterns and constellations are all there – Orion's Belt, the Big Dipper, the Little Dipper. I'm overwhelmed by how big the universe is; it's larger and more beautiful and harder to understand than I ever imagined. I'm a speck in the big universe, and each star is radiant against the night backdrop. The glimmering light reminds me of Will and how much I want to be next to him. It seems right to share this moment with him. He'd get it and understand how amazed I am at it all.

When I try to catch his eye, he turns toward me like he's been waiting, and our eyes lock. No one else notices. At least I don't think they do, but I don't care. Because when I look at Will, I see nothing but him, and he looks at me as if I'm his whole world. *Oh, wow, I like him. There's no denying it.*

I break our gaze. It's too much for me to stay that connected. I lie back on the blanket and exhale for a long time. As if someone lit a match inside me, way deep down, it's a long time before I can speak again.

Nadine's the one who suggests we go back. We gather our things and start down the hill. Darkness envelopes us, making me feel alone, and the cold brisk air forces me to take a couple of deep breaths.

Alex walks beside me the whole way down. Will walks alone. At the end of the dirt trail, I end up walking with Nadine. She's a whole head taller than me, and I feel small next to her, in all the ways a person can feel small. She's beautiful and perfect, and both her parents are alive. She's the one dating Will. They have history together. I'm just some girl he's restoring a lighthouse with. I play with the rings on my fingers and bite the inside of my lip. Maybe she found out about the lighthouse and is upset, because she doesn't say a word the whole way down.

We all part ways at Main Street. Alex and I are the only ones who live outside town. Although we shared that heart-stopping moment on that hill, Will doesn't say good-bye. I try to catch his eye, but he's not paying attention to me.

Alex, hands in his pockets, shuffles down the road in silence until we reach the woods. To the left is the coast and the lighthouse; the right leads to the farm and Alex's house.

I'm eager to get home, but Alex sidles closer and closer. He takes my hand and slows down. "Ellie, could we talk for a minute?" His voice is low and shaky.

I pause on the trail, not wanting to talk to Alex about anything important. I want to get back to Violet's and go to bed. "What's going on?" I try to sound interested.

He reaches for my face and tips my chin up. "It's just when we were on the stargazing hill, I wanted to do something, but didn't because everyone else was there." And then he leans forward like he intends to kiss me.

He is going to kiss me!

I tense up and move my head away. "Alex, it's late. I'd

better get to Violet's before she worries."

"Oh." His voice is laced with disappointment.

I reach for Alex's hand and tug him gently down the trail. "Let's hang out tomorrow, OK?"

Alex smiles, but his eyes flicker like he's trying hard to hide his disappointment. "Sure, Ellie."

My throat's tight. He's such a nice guy, and I hate hurting people's feelings. We go on for a few steps in dead, awkward silence.

Then, where the trail breaks into two paths, the old man appears, lit by the crescent moon.

I gasp and grip Alex's hand tighter. "Do you see that man?" I whisper.

The man's limping along in the opposite direction, his back toward us, but it's him.

"Ellie?" Alex says. "Are you all right?"

"Shh," I say. "I don't want him to see me. He freaks me out."

"Ellie, there's no one there. The trail's empty."

I point at the man. "He's right over there."

Alex shakes his head. "There's no one on this path. You're probably seeing a shadow or something."

I crinkle my brow. Am I imagining things? Then, the old man shifts toward me, and our eyes lock. My feet are plastered to the ground. I can't move. I only stare, and he stares back. Then he barely lifts his eyebrows, as if I've discovered a secret. I blink, and when I open my eyes again, he's gone. He's disappeared into the darkness like a vapor, leaving me with chills running up and down my back. I can't breathe. Did I see him, or not?

I try to get myself together. I worry I'm going crazy. I finally breathe in, run my hand over my cheek, disengage my hand from Alex's, and hug myself.

Alex puts an arm around me. "Ellie?" he whispers. "Are you all right?"

"Yeah." I rub my forehead. "I must be tired."

We quicken our pace. Alex keeps glancing back and

side to side like he's freaked out. I'm scared too. I didn't see a ghost, did I? Was the man actually there?

We say good-bye at our driveways, and Alex rushes home.

I go to the refrigerator and take out the glass bottle of milk, pour myself a cup, and heat it in the microwave. Violet and Ben's television is still on in their bedroom. I knock on the door and crack it open. They're perched on their bed, eating popcorn, and watching a movie.

"How were the stars?" Ben asks.

"All right," I tell him. "I'm going to bed now."

"You sleep well, honey," Violet says. "You want some popcorn?"

"No, thanks. I have some milk, and I'm ready for bed."

I go to the window seat. I have some thinking to do. What's the deal with the old man? And since when did I become someone who sees ghosts? I'm tempted to call Guadalupe. She knows all about weird things like that.

And why couldn't Alex see him?

But Will saw him, not just me.

Because I'm being honest, I'd better just get it out. I like Will. Really like him. I'm trying hard not to, because Nadine's interested in him, and I don't want to get caught in a love triangle drama. But the plain truth is, I like him.

At the beginning of the summer I expected this to be the worst summer of my life. I was wrong. So far—

One horse to ride
One old, rundown lighthouse to restore
One crazy dog
One very scary invisible man
One family who cares for me
And one guy named Will – who's flipped my world upside-down.

breakfast troubles

Even though I don't get much sleep, I wake early and hope that Will is still going to meet me at the cottage. I want to tell him about the old man. I leave a note for Violet. I grab a granola bar and a banana, and run out of the house. I whistle for Goldie. She comes like we've been friends for years, and we gallop to the lighthouse. Will is coming out of the woods when I arrive.

I don't wait. I spill everything. "Alex couldn't see the old man," I tell him. I climb off Goldie and get real serious. "When Alex and I came to the crossroads in the woods, the old man appeared out of thin air. He had his back to me and was walking to the coast. We didn't talk or anything, but he wasn't hiding either, and I saw him as clearly as if it were daylight." I pause. "At least I think I did."

Will just stares at me. I can't even see him breathing. I raise my eyebrows and tilt my head like I'm trying to make sure he's awake.

"Hello? I'm serious. Alex didn't see anything."

Will starts toward the lighthouse. "Did anything

happen with you and Alex last night?" His back is to me.

"I just told you. He walked me home, and we saw the old man. Or I saw the man, but Alex didn't. Are you listening to anything I'm saying?"

Will turns around and runs his hands through his hair. "Did anything else happen? You two didn't kiss or anything like that?"

"Of course not." I put my hands on my hips. "What is wrong with you? I'm telling you that Alex couldn't see the old man. I think the man must be invisible. The same man you and I have talked to at this very lighthouse. And all you can ask is if we kissed? Why in the world would I kiss Alex?"

Will shrugs. "You two were pretty close that's all. Amy even asked if anything was going on between you guys. She wondered if he was going to kiss you last night." He stares at the ground.

Why does he care? He has a girlfriend.

"Do you have the key? We should go inside and get started." Will's eyes are serious, calm, and maybe sad. It's hard to tell.

I pull the key out of my pocket. "You seemed pretty annoyed last night. Did you have a fight with Nadine or something?"

"I don't want to talk about last night."

"You're the one who brought it up," I say, unlocking the door. "Can we talk about the old man?"

"Yeah." He opens the door. "Are we the only ones who can see him?"

"I don't know. Don't you think it's weird that Alex couldn't see him and that the man just disappeared? Do you think I'm crazy?"

"No crazier than me, because I've seen him too. I wonder if he'll show up today."

I scour the landscape for a sign of him. "I need to feed Maggie." I take a large scoop of dog food from the bag inside the front door.

The trail is more prominent now and much easier to naviagate. Maggie comes to the edge of the cave and eats her food. Then she glances up at me, and for the first time, doesn't growl. She watches us for a minute or two, then lumbers inside her cave.

"See?" I elbow Will. "I told you she'd come around."

"Ellie, that dog is not going to come around. She's crazy."

"You need to have more faith. She'll be fine. She just needs time, that's all."

Back at the lighthouse, we scrub the outside. Will keeps sighing and glancing over his shoulder at me. Finally he throws his towel into the bucket full of dirty water.

"Ellie?" he asks. "Are you going to show the lighthouse to everyone?"

I'm holding a rag, standing on the ladder. "I hadn't really thought about it."

He grips his ladder. "Don't you think everyone would want to help?"

"I don't know. I kind of like just doing it with the two of us, you know? Sort of personal."

He goes back to scrubbing. "It's just that, well, I want them to know about us," he says, just loudly enough for me to hear.

I crinkle my eyes, thinking really hard. "What do you mean 'us'?"

"Never mind." He backs down the ladder, squeezes the washcloth into the bucket, picks up the ladder, and lugs it to the far side of the lighthouse. He scrubs the walls like they have graffiti on them. He keeps his lips pinched together and his eyes straight.

I stay on my ladder, but glance over at him every couple of minutes. I'm not sure what he means about 'us.' Our friendship is weird, that's true. And it might be better if Amy, Jake, and Alex, and even Nadine knew we were friends. But, I really want to keep the lighthouse a secret.

I'd like to find a way to the tell everyone we're friends without mentioning the lighthouse. I'm just about to ask Will if he has any ideas, but he gets down off the ladder, throws the rag into the bucket, and walks toward me. He runs his fingers through his hair and rubs his face like he needs to shave.

"OK, I'll tell you," he says real loudly. "Could you just

come down here for a minute?"

"What is your problem today?" I hang my rag on a ladder rung and descend.

"I broke up with Nadine last night. Or at least told her there's no chance of us getting together."

"Are you serious?"

"Yes.

"But she likes you so much."

"Ellie, the thing is... I like you. As more than a friend. I broke it off with Nadine, because I want to be honest."

"I... um... don't know what to say. I'm surprised. Really surprised."

I like Will, but it never occurred to me – and I mean never – that he might actually like me. The thought of going out with him, and the relationship going somewhere, scares me to death. It terrifies me to think of him that close.

"I'm... I'm not ready for a relationship. Can we just stay friends?"

"Sure, whatever." He turns back to washing the lighthouse walls and doesn't say anything for a long time. His silence makes me uneasy.

My stomach is nervous. My shoulders tense, and I don't know what to do. I don't want to lose his friendship. "You want to come back to the house for breakfast?" I ask.

He thinks for a minute. "Sure."

We set our tools inside the lighthouse. We're locking up when the old man comes over the ridge. He seems intent and purposeful, different from before. He normally wanders aimlessly, glancing about everywhere. But this morning he walks right toward us.

I step back, and Will reaches for my hand. I cling to it and move closer, which I'm not sure I should do, but I want his support. The old man comes near enough that sunspots are visible all over his face. He marches back and forth, staring at both of us.

"Stay away from that dog!" He brandishes his cane, and then instead of walking all the way down the path, he vanishes the way dew disappears when the sun warms the air.

"Did that guy just disappear?" Will asks, still holding my hand.

"That's exactly what happened last night. So, I'm not crazy. Not if you saw it too."

Will pulls me away from the lighthouse. "Ellie, let's not tell anyone we've seen someone who vanishes into thin air."

I agree with a quick nod. The whole thing is crazy. "You still hungry for breakfast?"

"Yes."

"Want to ride Goldie with me?"

He tilts his head and smiles. A cute I-know-what-you're-thinking smile. "Sure, why not?"

I take Goldie's reins and mount. Will gets on behind me. He fidgets, trying to find a spot for his arms. He places them on his legs, but when Goldie takes off, he wraps his arms around my waist and holds on. Despite how hard I'm fighting it, it feels right.

We dash down the trail for about a hundred yards. Then I slow Goldie, loosen up on the reins, and let her amble down the dirt road. The morning air smells fresh, and when the breeze blows just right, the scent of Will's soap, his cologne, make it hard to think straight.

Will keeps one arm around my waist but puts the other on his thigh. I lean back against him, and he breathes in slowly. "Your hair smells like the salt air and coconut."

He runs his hand down the length of my braid like it's a silk scarf. "Your hair is almost black."

"It must come from my dad. My mom's hair was blonde."

"When the sun hits it, I see tints of red." he says, gently.

"You have nice hair too," I tell him, and then I feel stupid. Did I really just tell him he had nice hair? "I mean, I like the color is all," I say under my breath.

"You sure you only want to be friends, Eleanor?" His lips brush the tip of my ear, sending goose bumps down my entire body.

"I'm sure," I say, shivering. "It scares me, is all."

"What are you so scared of?"

"I don't know. I mean, you just broke up with Nadine. I don't want to mess with that. Also, I realize that I'm not exactly the only girl you've ever liked. I don't want to be one of the girls you hardly remember." My voice trails off.

"I have a hard time imagining that I could ever forget you." He trails his hand down my left arm, raising more goose bumps.

"You'll forget me when the summer is over," I tell him. "I'll become a distant memory of some girl you restored a lighthouse with."

"Eleanor, you could never become anyone's distant memory."

"Let's talk about something else."

"OK." He runs his fingers over my hair again. A soothing touch. I don't draw away.

We reach my driveway. Alex is cutting into our side yard by the orchard. I wave. What's he going to say about Will and me riding together? The butterflies in my stomach flitter like crazy.

"Does Alex come over to your house a lot?" Will asks.

"No, but because he lives close, and mows the lawn, I'm not surprised he's here. He's becoming a friend."

"You sure have a lot of friends who'd like to be more than just friends."

I shake my head. "I do not." I turn around and stare at Will through the corner of my eye. "Just be nice to him, OK? Don't get all brooding and moody."

"I get brooding and moody?" He slides off the horse and helps me down.

"I can't be the first person who's ever mentioned it?"

"My mom, but she doesn't count."

"Just be nice." We walk toward the front porch. Alex meets us at the stairs. I motion for both of them to go around to the kitchen door.

"I wasn't expecting to see you here, Will," Alex says. "Everything OK?"

I pipe up. "Yeah, I invited him for breakfast."

We step into the kitchen. Ben is trying to get breakfast on the table and seems flustered. There's a blob of oatmeal on the floor. Ben holds up an empty bowl, and both twins look like they've been in trouble.

"Hi, Ben," I say, and motion for Will and Alex to come into the kitchen.

"Morning, Ellie. Your aunt is sleeping in this morning. She was up with Prissy, who threw up all night."

"Oh, that's too bad." I use a paper towel to clean up the oatmeal from the floor. "Have you eaten? Can I make you some breakfast?"

He shakes his head. "No, I have to run. Could you help with the boys while I check on Prissy?"

"Sure."

Ben hands me the empty bowl, and I give it to Will. "Could you get them more oatmeal, so I can get our eggs started?"

Alex is standing by the counter watching us with a surprised, deer-in-the-headlights look on his face. I didn't realize how different I was with Will when we're on our own. I guess our relaxed way with each other is obvious.

"What do you want me to do?" Alex glances back and forth from me to Will.

"Why don't you put in some toast? I'll make scrambled eggs. Mexican style. You do want breakfast, right?" I ask Alex.

"I could eat a little." He heads for the breadbox. I take eggs from the refrigerator, and Will pours more oatmeal into a bowl and adds hot water. He turns the spoon slowly, then points it at me. I raise my eyebrows and try not to laugh.

Alex moves closer to me. "Ellie, I came over early because I wanted to make sure you were all right after last night." He shifts his eyes back and forth as if he doesn't want Will to know what we're talking about.

I crack the eggs into the frying pan and don't look up. "I'm fine. Sorry I got so spooked."

"You sure you're OK?"

"I'm fine, really." I force myself to look at him.

None of us say anything for a minute while the eggs crackle and the intensity in the air bubbles around us. When the eggs are done, I set them on the table, get some juice out of the fridge, and we all sit down to eat.

Afterwards, the twins beg to watch a cartoon. I walk them into the family room, and they sit on the floor in front of the TV. When I return, the guys are still quiet. Alex and Will are staring at each other, like they're having a conversation without words.

"Ellie, are you going swimming today?" Alex finally asks.

I shake my head. "I doubt it, not with Aunt Violet being so tired. Maybe I can go when the twins take their naps."

"OK." Alex finishes his toast, stands, and tells Will he'll see him at the café.

Once he's out the door, I glare at Will. "Nice job."

"What?" He tilts his chair back on two legs. "I was quiet, but I tried not to act moody."

"Alex is going to think something is going on between us. I didn't want him to get the wrong idea."

He picks up his plate. "Something is going on between us, Ellie. You're just a 'little scared,' remember?"

I stand. "Just because I'm the only girl who wants to be friends with you doesn't mean I'm afraid."

He starts cleaning the plates and putting them in the dishwasher, but then turns to me. "Eleanor Martinson, you're the one who said you were afraid, I didn't come up with that on my own. Remember? On the horse?"

Heat seeps into my face and neck. Will takes my hand and steps toward me until we're only inches apart. "That's all right. I'm not going anywhere." Then he lets me go and turns back to the sink. "Don't forget we both see the same invisible guy. It might be a sign or something."

I stare out the kitchen window. I don't want to let him see my eyes because I am afraid. So afraid. He is the cutest guy, the most intense, and the hardest to understand. I don't want to get hurt, and I don't want to let myself feel so strongly for him. If I unlock my heart even a little, I'll feel a lot more for him than I can handle. And I can't afford any more heartache right now.

He puts the last dish in the dishwasher, and I wipe down the table. The kids watch their show. I don't say anything.

"Thanks for breakfast, Eleanor," Will says as we finish.

"Why do you keep calling me 'Eleanor'?"

He steps closer and strokes my cheek. "I like your name." He turns to the door. "If you want to come to the lake and need to bring the boys, I'll swim with them."

The summer breeze blows into the house when Will opens the door. His hair lifts in the wind. I watch until he disappears from sight.

He likes me. I can't believe it. I stand there, letting it soak in. Then, I remember Alex. What's he going to tell everyone about me and Will?

A few minutes later, Violet stumbles downstairs. Her hair is straggly, hanging in clumps. The bags under her eyes look like she got beaten up, and her face is pasty. She's wearing dirty pajamas and smells like a bathroom. She seems so unlike herself that I shudder when she comes into the kitchen. She covers her mouth with her hand and whispers, "I have the flu. Don't come close."

"Do you want me to take the boys out for the day? I could take them to Amy's."

"Julie's coming over." Violet forces out each word.

"Are you sure? I don't mind watching them."

"I'm sure. I did this for her kids a couple of times when they were little. But you should go to Amy's. Maybe stay the night. I don't want you to get sick."

"I'll go for the day, but I don't want to stay overnight."

She totters to the counter and grabs the edge.

I wonder if she'll throw up right there on the kitchen floor.

"Can you watch the boys until Julie gets here?" She closes her eyes and holds her breath.

"Absolutely. I'll call later today to see how everything is going."

"Sounds good." She staggers up stairs, gripping the rail.

I go into the family room and read a book to the twins. Then I take them outside, and we goof off on their swing set. They keep making throw-up noises, and it's grossing me out.

Julie drives down the driveway. She parks and takes

out a duffle bag. How long does she plan on staying?

"Hey, Ellie." She waves and slams the car door with her hip. "You're not sick too, are you?"

"No, I'm fine so far. I don't really think I should leave Violet though."

"Yes, you should, honey. You head over to my house. Amy'll hang out with you. I'm going to stay the night to help Ben, and you're more than welcome to stay over at our house."

"I'll come home after dinner," I tell her.

"Amy would love to have you. She wants to ask you something about this weekend, I think."

We say good-bye, and I pack some things for the day. I don't want to stay the night. I like the privacy of my room. And I don't want to be that close to Will. I'm afraid I'll let it slip that I like him too.

an invitation

At the café, Will's making a latte for a customer. I slip through the door, trying to be as inconspicuous as possible. I don't want him to get the idea I want to be with him.

"Ellie?" he asks. "Did you see my mom?"

"Yes. She's come to the rescue. It's not just Prissy who's sick. Violet is too. I've been banished to your house. Amy's supposed to take care of me."

He raises his eyebrows. "I can take care of you."

I try to hide my smile. "Very funny. Where's Amy?"

"She's upstairs. I think she wants to go swimming."

"I brought my suit. You coming?"

"I have to work now that my mom has gone to your house."

I shrug. "Sorry. I'll see you later, all right?"

"You could come down and hang out with me." He gives me his blue-eyed stare.

I duck my head and try to hide my interest. "I should spend the day with Amy. We haven't had much time together lately."

I run up the stairs and knock on her door. She opens it and, when she realizes it's me, she pulls me in like she's been waiting weeks and weeks for me to get there.

"Jake just called and told me that when Alex went to your house this morning, you and Will were riding the horse together, and Will had his hands all over you."

I cringe. "He was holding on so he wouldn't fall off the horse."

"Ellie, is something going on between you and my brother?"

"No." My voice is very serious. "I mean we've hung out a few times. He's seen me around a few times, and we've talked. But that doesn't mean anything is going on."

"You and Will, huh?" She studies me. "I can see why he likes you."

"You can? I can't." Then I quickly add, "Besides nothing going on between us. We're just friends." I'm not about to tell her we've been hanging out every day for a few weeks.

She furrows her eyebrows. "I thought something was going on with you and Alex. He always sits next to you at the lake, and last night he walked you home. Are you working it with two guys?"

My goodness! How do these things happen? I push my hair back. "I'm not working it with anyone," I tell her. "Alex walked me home because he lives next door to me. And I told you, Will and I are just friends."

"I think it's cute that you're the quietest girl this town has ever seen, and my brother, who's never had to pursue anyone, is caught riding a horse with you. And Alex, who's never liked any girl, is totally jealous. It must be your mysterious air."

Mysterious air? "Can we talk about something else?" I ask.

"Sure," she says. "Actually there's something I wanted to talk to you about. Let's go to my room."

After she closes the door, she sits on the bed, and runs

her fingers through her hair. "Ellie, I'm going to my dad's this weekend. I was wondering if you'd like to come to Seattle with me."

My heart beats faster. I haven't been back to the city since my mom died.

"How long are you going to be there?" My stomach's already swirling into a whirlpool of anxiety.

"Just for the weekend." She pulls her hair to one side of her neck and changes her playlist. "My brother is furious he has to go. He promised my dad he'd go home for one weekend this summer. They aren't talking, you know."

I scrunch up my eyes in confusion. "Who's not talking?"

"Will and my dad. Or should I say, Will's not talking to my dad. But they made some deal, so he has to go."

"They aren't talking at all?" I knew Will was mad at his dad, but I didn't realize they weren't talking.

"Will is still mad at my dad for leaving my mom. My dad lives with someone else, and Will hates her. Absolutely hates her. I don't get it. Christine is one of the prettiest women ever. Besides she makes my dad happy."

I don't say anything for a minute, but all I can think is how much it sucks to be her mom. "Don't you feel bad for your mom?"

Amy glances over and shrugs. "Mom gave up. She didn't fight for my dad or anything. She just walked away. I would have fought harder."

I need to steer the conversation back to her original question. "Amy, thanks for the invitation, but I don't think I'll be able to go."

She frowns. "Why not? My dad is the nicest man in the world, and you can see the house where I live during the year." She gets this pleading look in her eyes.

"I'll think about it."

"We can go shopping downtown for school clothes and get our hair done. Please come, Ellie."

I bite my lip and assure her I'll let her know later. But

I'm not going.

Finally we go to the lake. When Jake and Alex show up, Amy tells them we're going to Seattle. I don't want her to think I'm weird or that I'm blowing her off, but I don't want to go back to Seattle. I'll have to return at the end of the summer, but that's with Jose, and to my own trailer. Hard, yes. Alone, no.

Later, I go to the lighthouse, and Will is there, waiting for me on the cottage steps. He doesn't smile when I walk up. He's resting his chin on his hand, staring at the ground.

"I didn't expect you to be here." My voice is warm.

"I texted Amy, and she said you'd left the lake. I figured you'd come here afterwards."

"Everything OK?" I ask. His voice is quieter. Something seems off.

"Did my sister invite you to go with us for the weekend?" he asks.

I don't want to talk about this. "Yeah, she mentioned it, but I don't think I'm going."

He sits up. "I figured."

I glance over at the water. "I want to keep working on the lighthouse."

"Ellie," he says, in this low voice. "I was hoping you'd come."

I pull the key out of my pocket, trying not to look him in the eye. "Why?"

He steps closer to me. "I'd like you to meet my friends and stuff."

I'd better tell him the truth, or he'll keep bugging me about it. "It's just that I haven't been to Seattle since my mom..."

He gently squeezes my shoulder. Then he brushes wisps of hair from my face. "I'll be there with you."

My heart flutters. It makes me nervous. "I'm not sure, Will."

"Ellie, it's not just that I want to introduce you to my friends. I'd like you to be there, so I'm not so alone." His voice is quiet, almost a whisper.

I catch a sadness in his tone I haven't heard before. "Amy says you two don't talk much? You and your dad, I mean."

"We don't talk at all."

I unlock the door to the lighthouse, and we go inside. It's more like a cottage now. We've made it inviting since we cleaned the windows, removed the sheets from the furniture, and dusted everything. Will's hand brushes mine as he walks past. I'm not sure if it was on purpose or by accident? Either way, it makes my throat tighten.

We climb to the balcony and sit beside each other.

I touch his hand. "Why would you feel alone in your own house?"

He stares at the water. "It's a long story." He stiffens. "Listen, if you don't want to go I understand. It's just that it's complicated with my dad is all."

I wrap my hand around his and squeeze gently. "I never met my dad. I don't even know who he is."

Will stays quiet, and I wonder if he even heard me. "I hate my dad," he says, without looking at me.

I'm not sure how to respond, or even if he wants me to. But I know all about hate. It's poison. Memories push their way to the forefront of my mind... I close my eyes for a moment, regret filling me like a faucet turned on.

I speak, but my voice comes out quietly, and there's an ache in it. "I remember the first time I ever said that about my mom. I still feel guilty about it."

"Why? What happened?"

The day comes back, forming in my mind. I try to swallow, but my throat's so tight, and all I want to do is run away and ignore this memory, but part of me wants to tell him something real about my mom. I start quiet and slow...

"I was probably only ten or eleven. It was the first night in more than a month she wasn't going to work. I wanted to hang out, watch a movie or something." Just thinking about it makes everything inside me ache.

"I even cleaned the trailer so she wouldn't have anything to complain about. After dinner, she went to her room. 'You don't mind if I go out, do you, honey?' she asked, coming down the hall."

She was fluffing her hair, and she'd put on these huge silver loop earrings. God, she looked bad. She was always trying too hard.

"I was washing the dishes. She patted me on the back on her way past. 'Don't wait up, El,' she said."

My voice cracks, and I have to stop. Will waits quietly, but I hardly see him, it's like I'm still standing there at the kitchen sink, biting my lip to fight the tears, and washing those dishes so hard I practically scrubbed the skin off my fingers. I must have been trying to scrub away all the fury and frustration. Later when I passed a mirror, I noticed my bottom lip had my teeth marks on it.

I graze my finger across my lip, and that brings me back to Will. He squeezes my fingers like he wants me to go on, but he doesn't say anything.

"Later that night she stumbled into the trailer. A man's voice shushed her." I close my eyes for a second. I want to get up and run out of the lighthouse, but I force myself to stay. To remember. To tell the story.

"In the morning... I crept out of my bedroom."

The stale cigarette smoke, the beer cans scattered across the coffee table are etched in my memory, like a carving.

"My mom's door was open, and the man was belting his jeans, about to hightail it out of there before she even woke up." What a jerk.

"When he saw me, he jumped so hard the entire trailer shook. He picked up his cowboy hat and hurried to the front door. 'You're cute, kid,' he said. 'Go in and take care of your mom. She's gonna need it.'"

A few moments later, his truck engine revved loudly enough to wake the whole trailer park. But he was right.

My mom needed to be cared for. That's all I ever did. I always took care of her. Until I stopped.

"What happened after he left?" Will's voice is soft, but he's there, hanging on every word.

"I went back to check on my mom. She looked old lying there. Her mascara was running down her face. She'd want a glass of water and aspirin when she came to, so I went into the kitchen and got out a cup. I'm not even sure who I was talking to, but words rushed out of me like I was defending myself in a courtroom or something, 'I can't do this anymore. I hate her, I just hate her.' As soon as I said it, I wished I hadn't, but I didn't know how to fix it. Any of it. The whole thing seemed so messed up."

When I finish the story, I glance over at Will and take deep breaths. "That was the first time I ever said I hated her." I hang my head, sorrow and guilt pooling inside of me, rising, rising.

He doesn't say anything for a minute, and his silence soothes me, giving me a minute to push my guilt back down.

Then, he asks the question I can't answer, "What do you mean, *the first time*?" His eyes are warm and kind, but they have this edge that demands honesty.

I pinch my lips together. I can't go there. I won't go there. Not now.

I think he understands, because he nods and gently slides his arm around my shoulders, drawing me toward him until we're touching. I lay my head against his chest, and we watch the water for a few minutes.

It's the first time I've ever told anyone that story. Being with Jose made everything easy, because he knew my mom, and he knew what was going on. With Will, I have to share my history. I have to tell my story if I want him to know it.

And the truth is, it doesn't matter how many times we say we hate our parents. It's not true. We just wish it could've been better. Deep down, even though Will is angry at his dad and I was devastated by my mom, the truth is we both would do just about anything to change how things turned out.

Does Will feel guilty for saying he hates his dad? He doesn't seem to. He seems angry.

He breaks the silence. "Do you want to go and check on Maggie?"

"Sure."

We climb down and step outside the cottage. The sun's brightness forces me to squint. The salt air smells clean and calms my swirling emotions. Will reaches over and winds his fingers through mine, keeping me close. I like his nearness.

Maggie doesn't growl when we stand outside her cave. I know better than to go too close, so I set down food and talk to her, trying to reassure her.

Afterwards Will and I stand outside the lighthouse facing each other, his fingers still entwined with mine.

"Thanks for telling me that story, Ellie," Will says quietly. And then he gathers me into his arms, and, exhaling slowly, I let him wrap me up. Tears well in my eyes as I rest my cheek on his shoulder. The skin underneath his shirt is hot against my face.

"Are you going to come this weekend?" he asks.

I can't say no to him. Not now. "I'll talk to my aunt."

Violet's whole body tightens up, and her face falls when I tell her I thinking about going to Amy's for the weekend. She's normally opinionated, but calm. At dinner, there's no peace, only tension.

Prissy drops her fork.

Violet reaches down and grabs it. "Be careful, Prissy." Her voice is sharp and tense.

I stay quiet, staring at my food.

After dinner, Violet goes to her room. Finally, when

I'm washing the dishes, she comes back into the kitchen.

"Ellie, I can't deny I don't really want you going," she admits. "Are you and Amy even close? Or is this about Will?"

"Amy invited me, and it'll be a good chance to get to know her better. Will also asked me to go." I shrug, trying to downplay my feelings for him.

Violet pinches her lips, and her face gets serious. "Are you sure you're ready to go to Seattle? I'm glad you're friends with Amy, and I know you and Will have been getting to know each other, but I don't want you to go too soon."

I'm standing near the counter, towel-drying one of the big bowls from our salad. I don't want her know that I'm more worried than she is. I just say, "I like Amy and she wants me to meet her dad."

"But you want to go, right?" She rests her hand on the counter, and her eyes narrow in on me.

"Sure, why wouldn't I?" I've never had any adult this interested in my plans, and I'm not sure how to react.

"I know you'd be fine going with them for the day, but are you ready to go for the weekend?"

No matter what I say, I won't convince her.

"It's only two nights." I set the plate I'm drying on the counter and try to sound confident. "I'll call you Saturday, and you can make sure I'm OK."

She places her hand on my cheek. "Ellie, you don't have to worry about me. It's *you* I'm worried about."

I assure her I'll be fine, and I almost believe it myself, but during the night I toss and turn. I can't shake the feeling that maybe I'm not ready to go away for the weekend. Despite the new relationship I have with my aunt, I feel safe in her house, and I'm not sure I'll feel secure in Seattle for two days, even if I am with Will.

ferry rides and tension

Will picks me up in his Subaru. The silver paint glistens in the morning sun, and I sigh. I don't want my emotions to ruin the day before it even starts.

Will opens the trunk for my bag, and when I set it inside, his fingers graze the back of my hand. He doesn't look at me, so I'm not completely sure it was intentional.

Once we're on the road, the stark silence makes it clear something is wrong between Amy and Will. Will's staring out the windshield, hands planted on the wheel at ten and two as if he's taking his driver's test, and Amy fiddles with the music, completely ignoring me.

It isn't until later, when Amy and I are alone on the ferry, that she lightens up and finally talks to me. Will, on the other hand, is still acting as cool and reserved as he did when I got in the car. I thought he wanted me to go on this trip.

Amy and I go to the opposite side of the ferry where no wind ruffles our hair. She's worried hers'll get all messed up. We rest against the railing and watch for orcas. One rolls up out of the water and somersaults back under.

"You're going to love my dad's house." Amy puts her arm through mine. "He has hundreds of movies. We can stay up all night."

"Sounds like fun." I'm hardly listening to her. My stomach is doing somersaults of its own, but not as rhythmically as the orcas. The last time I went on a ferry was with Aunt Violet on our way to her house. I study the sparkling water and force myself to concentrate on other things. I don't want to think about my mom.

"Should we check on your brother?" I suggest.

"No," she says. "He's mad at me right now. It's not worth trying to talk to him."

"What did you two fight about?" I shield my eyes from the bright sun.

She flips her hair out of her face. "I told him to stay away from you this weekend. He has this habit of fooling around with my friends, and I told him he wasn't allowed to come near you." She lifts her chin in a defiant attitude.

Her words sink in. She needs to know about Will and me. I put my arms over the railing and let them dangle out over the water to avoid looking at her straight on. "Amy, the thing is…Will and I are friends. We've hung out together a few times this summer."

This is exactly why Will wanted them to know about us. Doubt swims inside my already swirling stomach.

She freezes, and her eyes turn dark and serious. "Don't tell me you're crushing on my brother. You're supposed to be *my* friend." Her face is tight, and she's clenching the railing.

Amy's the one who invited me, but I'm on this ferry because Will asked me to come. I'm stuck. I take a big breath. "I came here to be with you. But Will is my friend too."

Amy shakes her head. "My brother doesn't do friendship with girls. He's a player."

I frown. "He does friendship with me."

"Maybe, but the question is: for how long?"

I don't have an answer. I have no idea what might happen with Will, but her question looms in my mind.

We step out of the wind and the bright sun into the seating area. It smells old and plasticky. People mill around, shoving coins into vending machines. There's a family with three little kids begging to go up to the high deck. At the café, a long line of people wait to order coffee. When we stroll past, I catch the faint aroma of fresh coffee grounds.

Off in a corner, Will's engrossed in some thick book with worn and yellowed pages. It looks like he bought it at a thrift store. I stare hard, hoping he'll feel my gaze. His eyes flick up from the page and then over at me. I give a half-wave. He smiles but, after a brief glance at Amy, turns back to his book.

A few seconds later, Will saunters over. "I'm going down to the car." His voice is tight, almost mad.

I stand. "Should we all go?"

Amy shakes her head. "I'm going to get a latte first. Ellie, do you want one?"

I'd really like a moment alone with Will to see if he's all right. "There are a lot of people waiting to get lattes. I think I'll just go back down to the car."

"If you're sure." Amy's voice is annoyed, and she shoots a glare at Will before she gets in line.

Will and I head for the staircase.

"Sorry about your fight with Amy," I say, hoping he's not annoyed with me.

He reaches for my hand. "Your secret lighthouse is making it hard to tell people I care about you."

I gulp. My face heats.

His Subaru is at the front of the line. Will unlocks the front passenger side for me.

I shake my head. "I should sit in the back so your sister can sit here."

"No, you shouldn't. Sit next to me."

Once we're inside, he gently runs his hand over my rings and fingers through my bracelets as if counting them. "What's with the number seven?"

"You noticed?" I'm surprised. No one has ever noticed before. Not even Jose.

"Yeah. What's with it?"

I lower my head and stare at the seat. "I read somewhere that seven is the number for being complete, whole. I guess I'm trying to figure out how to become whole." My heart aches telling him this secret. I'm so far away from feeling whole it's not even in the cards anymore.

He plays with my palm, not saying anything.

***

When we get to the house, it's obvious by the girlfriend's face that neither Amy nor her dad said anything about me coming. Amy introduces me.

I don't think I should be here.

Christine is as tall and thin as a model and has long, silken hair. She dresses like she owns her own store brand. "Ellie, right?" she asks when we step inside as if Amy didn't just introduce me.

I nod.

"This isn't a farmhouse in the country." Her tone is sweet like fake maple syrup, but underneath there's tightly controlled anger.

Their house is gigantic and elegant. The kind of house where people get lost.

Will steps forward before I have a chance to say anything. "She's not stupid, Christine. She won't want to touch your stuff." He looks at her like she's a wicked witch, and he's busy plotting how to throw water on her, so she'll melt.

Christine smiles at Will, but her eyes are so hateful, I flinch. "Of course. We're glad you're here."

"Thanks," I mumble, wishing for the comfort of Aunt Violet's messy house. Even with the unexpectedness of my arrival, I never once felt like I was in the way there.

Amy explains, "Christine is an interior designer, and she's made the house absolutely beautiful. She worries we'll mess it up. I promise, Christine, we'll be careful." Amy stares at Christine like she's a goddess come down from heaven.

Will scowls at his sister. "Thanks for the speech, Amy. We all know how much she *looooved* redecorating our house."

Amy ignores Will and motions me through the kitchen, which is the size of my entire trailer. This is not where I belong. At all. In the living room, spacious French doors reveal a swimming pool, lawn chairs facing the view of the water, and a long dock on Lake Washington.

I trail behind Amy as she climbs the stairs. Will follows and slips into his room. Amy's pink and white room has more pillows than Violet has in her whole house.

"I'm glad to be home." Amy drops her bag on the floor. "I have much more room for my stuff and way more freedom than I have with my mom. Mom makes us work, clean our rooms, and cook, but here I pretty much do whatever I want."

This room looks like it's set for a stage. The curtains match the pillows, and the rug on the bedside carpet coordinates with the color of the lamp. The whole room looks like a magazine layout – completely fake. I scrunch my eyebrows and trace the edge of Amy's desk with one finger. "You'd rather live with your dad than your mom?"

"Yeah, I prefer the city, and I have a lot more space here." She lies back on her bed, but then sits up, setting a pillow in her lap. "I only stay with my mom during the summer."

"When did your parents get divorced?" I sit on the edge of her bed, hoping I don't wrinkle it or anything.

"Couple of years ago." Amy stares at the pillow, her

face serious. "I got over it pretty fast. Will's causing all the problems."

Everything about Amy screams that she's trying to be over it, but there's a look in her eyes, a disconnectedness or something, that affirms the opposite. "It's sad how angry Will is at your dad, isn't it? It must be hard."

"Will needs to learn to get along with everyone and make it work. My dad is with Christine. That's all there is to it."

I stare at her for a minute not sure what to say.

She squirms and says, "Want to go swimming before dinner?"

"That sounds good." I go into the bathroom that's connected with Amy's room to change. It's seriously like a hotel suite. When I step out, Amy hands me a towel, and I wrap it around my waist.

When we pass the kitchen, Christine is rubbing lemon and garlic onto salmon.

Amy beckons me toward the French doors, and we sneak out unnoticed. I take it Amy doesn't want to help Christine with dinner.

We toss our towels onto some lawn chairs.

"Are you going to swim or just lie out in the sun?"

Amy raises her eyebrows. "How about we do both?"

"Let's swim first. I'm hot."

While Amy pulls her hair back into a knot, I dive in. Then she jumps, gripping the side of the pool, so her hair doesn't get wet.

When I resurface, Will is staring at me through his window. I wave, inviting him down. He shakes his head, but I scrunch up my face like I'll be mad if he doesn't do what I'm asking. He nods and disappears from the window.

Amy's treading water off to the side. I don't even want to see if she's giving me a dirty look.

A few minutes later, Will appears at the French doors without a shirt on. I gulp and try to act disinterested, but man, he's good-looking.

Will dives in and comes up next to me. He splashes me, and I splash him back.

Finally Amy says, "Hey, you two. Your silence is as loud as a concert." Her sarcastic tone makes my stomach hurt. She climbs out.

Will clears his throat. "Amy, come back in the water."

"Just promise you two won't make me feel like the wobbly wheel on a tricycle." She sits by the edge of the pool and dangles her legs in the water.

I stay quiet.

All of a sudden, Will's face stiffens.

A man is stepping out of the French doors.

"Daddy," Amy calls. She hops up, grabs her towel, and runs over to him. He hugs her, but instead of looking at her, his eyes stop on Will.

"Will, good to see you. Last I heard, you weren't sure you were coming."

His hair is almost the same color as Will's. He has that same aloof air about him that Will's got.

"I changed my mind." Will gets out of the pool, takes one of the towels, and dries his face and chest. Instead of hugging his dad, he holds out his hand. They shake, then Will says, "I'm going to change for dinner."

His dad glances at the kitchen entry. "Christine said dinner'll be ready in a few minutes. We'll eat out here." He points to an outdoor glass table. He's wearing the kind of clothes Christine probably dressed him in.

Does Will's dad even know I'm here? Amy glances over at me, and her eyes light up like she's just remembered me. I get out of the water and wrap my towel around my waist.

Amy says, "Dad, this is my friend Ellie. She's here for the weekend too."

Amy's dad smiles and extends his hand. "Hi, Ellie. I'm so glad Amy brought a friend from the island."

"Thank you for having me, sir. Your home is beautiful."

I try to think of something better to say, but all I can think about is the fact that he left warm, friendly Julie for the lady who told me not to touch anything in her newly decorated home. I get that men like beautiful women, but I bet Julie was a better wife.

"You're welcome anytime," he says.

He brings Amy closer and kisses her head. "You'd never believe how much I miss you when you're gone."

"I miss you too, Daddy." Amy squeezes him around the waist. "But I'm having a good summer." She opens her blue eyes and stares at him like a little girl in love with her dad.

Something about this whole situation gives me an uneasy feeling.

Amy's dad cups his hands around her cheeks. "Does this have to do with that boy, Jake, you've been telling me about?"

Amy's eyes sparkle, and she wiggles out of his arms. "Maybe... and meeting Ellie. I've had fun with Ellie. I'm even jumping off the rope swing. Can you believe it?"

He ruffles her hair. "Wow! That's a real accomplishment for you." He turns toward me. "Now, Ellie, do I know your parents?"

I clear my throat. "I'm staying with Ben and Violet Parker." I'm not sure what else to say. "She's my aunt," I add.

He studies me. "Your mom was Rose?"

My eyes widen with surprise. I nod.

He stares off in the distance for just a second "I heard she died." He looks me in the eye. "I'm so sorry. It was terrible what happened."

I stare at the cement patio, shocked into silence that he knows. "Thank you," I force myself to say. My voice sounds hoarse, damaged.

After a few seconds of silence, I point toward the house. "Amy, I'm going up to change. I'll be down in a minute."

How does he know about my mom? Were they friends?

I run upstairs, trying to control the surge of emotions. I change in Amy's room, towel-dry my hair, and put on a pair of shorts and a T-shirt. I tie a hoodie around my waist in case I get cold.

I can't help but think about how Will treated his father. Amy acted like a mesmerized little girl when she saw him. Weird how two people can react to their own father in such opposite ways.

family fight

Will's music is blaring through his door. Part of me wants to knock and see how he's doing and why he walked away from his dad. But I'm not sure how to approach the subject. My hands tremble a little.

Instead of knocking, I pause with my hand on the door handle. I stay a second too long. Will opens his door and almost bumps into me. I jerk my hand back, clear my throat, and twist the hair tie off my wrist. I pull my hair in a ponytail in one swift move.

Will's eyes dance, and he grins at me. "Were you going to invite yourself in before dinner?"

I stare at the cream-colored carpet for a second. "No, I was going to see how you are."

He touches my arm like he's trying to reassure me. "I'm good. Do you want to see my room?" He reaches behind me and runs his hand over my ponytail. "Why do you always keep your hair up? I like it down."

I pull off the hair tie and shake out my hair, letting it flow down my back.

"Well, do you want to see my room or not?" He holds the door ajar, waiting for my response.

"We should probably go down for dinner."

He frowns. "I want you to see my space."

I'm nervous about being alone in his room. "I don't want Amy to get mad."

"Don't worry about Amy." He pulls me closer.

My face burns. "I don't want her to think I came here to be with you. I'm here because she invited me. I told her that you and I are just friends."

"Are we just friends?"

I step inside because Will's holding my hand, and I don't want to disappoint him. I ignore his question and focus on his tan walls and signed movie and book posters. "Was this always your room?"

"Yeah. When Christine wanted to redecorate it, I said no."

I walk to his bookshelf and run my fingers across a few of titles. "We've read so many of the same novels."

He stands closer than normal and puts a hand on my upper back, resting it over my hair.

I take a deep breath and try to concentrate, but all I can think about is his closeness. My stomach swirls, and my heart speeds up. "We should probably go downstairs for dinner," I whisper.

"Ellie?" he says, his breath soft against my ear.

"Hmm?" I stiffen a bit. *What am I doing?* He smells good, fresh like. I rest against him.

He puts his arm around my waist and nestles his lips against my neck, moving my hair back with his other hand. It feels good. I want him close, but I'm nervous because Amy called him a player. Jose has always told me not to believe half the romantic stuff guys say. It's because they want something, he says.

"Ellie, I'm glad you came this weekend. I didn't want to come alone."

"Why?" I arch my neck so he can nuzzle it more fully.

I shiver.

"Are you trembling?" he whispers.

I panic. I shift away and take a step toward the door. "We should go down for dinner." I avert my eyes. "I'm hungry, aren't you?"

He shakes his head and reaches for my hand. "Not for food."

"Well, I am." I take my hair tie off my wrist and put my hair into a ponytail again. "I'll see you downstairs."

Will doesn't say anything.

Did I hurt his feelings, or is he laughing at me? "I really feel like we should just be friends."

He steps nearer and stares into my eyes. "You're one of the best friends I've had in a long time. I don't want to hurt our friendship either, but I like you, and I don't want to pretend. I've been doing that all summer, Eleanor."

"My name is Ellie," I remind him. "What happens if we break up? Then we won't be friends anymore."

"You're breaking it off before it starts."

I hold out my hands in resignation. "We'd break up, and then we'd stop being friends. I can't take that right now. No more heartache."

"Ellie," he says. "I've never met a girl like you before. I don't know what to do with my feelings."

"Let's just stay friends for a while."

"How long is a while?" He shakes his head. "Never mind. Just answer one question. Do friends hold hands and kiss?"

I raise one eyebrow. "No. Well, maybe they can hold hands." I tighten my hands into fists at my side and then release them. "But that's all." I try to sound disinterested, but I press my lips together and can't help but wonder how his lips would feel on mine.

"Oh, really?" He moves toward me, his head tilted as if he's going to kiss me. I swallow.

But before he can, Amy's voice from downstairs pierces the moment. It's time for dinner.

I duck out of Will's room, my face hot, and hurry downstairs, trying to gain some modicum of poise. When I reach the landing, I glance back at Will. He's standing in the doorway of his room staring at me as if he sees deep into every part of me.

This is getting complicated. What if he breaks my heart?

A few weeks ago, he and I were having fun fixing up the lighthouse. Now, my heart is filled with conflicting emotions every time I see him, and I can barely hold back all my feelings for him.

Amy's probably right. He was fooling around with Nadine just few weeks ago. Someone like Will is too dangerous. *Don't kiss him*, I tell myself as I hurry into the kitchen.

Amy's balancing the salad bowl and three different dressings. I take the salad utensils from her and follow her onto the patio.

Christine's wearing a halter-top and a simple wraparound skirt. Her skin glistens in the evening, and she and Mr. Larson are holding hands. He's drinking a beer. Christine has a Bloody Mary.

Will finally joins us. His mischievous smile has disappeared, leaving his face hard and emotionless. With me, he was caring and present. But with his family, he's stone. The wall he's built around himself when he talks to Christine or his dad is almost visible.

As Will sits down, Mr. Larson carefully untangles his hand out of Christine's and hands me the green salad. "Ellie, would you like some?"

"Thank you."

I smile, and Mr. Larson takes a deep breath. But the family tension fills the air.

Amy sits silently for a moment. She's fiddling with her napkin, like she's not sure what to do with herself. Finally, she starts chatting with Christine about getting her hair cut that weekend. "No one in that small town knows what

I need done with my hair." She runs her fingers down the sides of her head.

Christine touches her own hair as if she wants to make sure it's not been subjected to small town hairdressers. "I'll call Mikal after dinner to see if he can fit you in tomorrow morning."

"Great. Maybe we can take Ellie to Westlake afterwards to do some shopping?" Amy cuts into her planked salmon, takes a bite, and then raises her eyebrows at me like she wants to make sure I'm interested in shopping.

"Whatever works." I take a bite of salad. "I'm just excited to be here."

Mr. Larson turns to Will. "Why don't we take the boat out in the morning? We haven't gone out on her for a long time."

Will doesn't even lift his head. "I have plans to see some of my friends."

Mr. Larson waits for a moment. "They're welcome to come along. I know how much you love to be out on the water. It was always your favorite place."

"Yeah, well, not anymore." His voice is quiet, tense. He takes a bite of his salmon and stares into the distance.

That must be why he loves the lighthouse. The water.

Christine sets her fork down and pinches her lips together. She points a finger at Will. "I'd appreciate it if you showed a little more respect to your father in his own house."

Amy gulps in a quick breath.

Mr. Larson places his hand on Christine's shoulder. "Don't worry about it, Chris. I understand if Will has other things to do."

"Are you kidding me?" she says. "He doesn't have anything else to do. He just likes to punish you with his hatred, don't you, Will?"

Will stares wide-eyed as he bites into a piece of bread. I can't believe it.

Mr. Larson speaks up again. "Christine, that's

enough."

"No, it's not." Christine takes a long sip of her drink, then slams it down. Red liquid sloshes out of the top of the glass and puddles around her plate. "I'm sick of his attitude, Ken." She thrusts her chair back and shakes a finger in Will's face. "In case you've forgotten, he is your father and pays for most of your existence. When you are in this house, you will respect him – or you can get out."

Will arches back and raises his arms, palms out, to show he isn't about to lose control. He flashes a big smile, puts his bread down, and slowly moves his eyes to meet her gaze. "Just the permission slip I needed. I think I'll get out." He stands, but Mr. Larson puts out his hand.

"Please, Will. Don't leave. I really want to see you this weekend."

Christine gasps. "Ken. Don't you dare take his side on this."

"Christine, this is my son. He's not the paperboy who threw the paper in the wrong spot on our front lawn. We can't just fire him."

Wouldn't want to be her paperboy, that's for sure.

"Oh, for God's sake," she says. She grimaces and hatred reverberates off her as she glares at Will. "You've done everything you possibly could to screw up my happiness with your dad since the day we decided to be together. But it's not going to work. We're together, Will. At some point you'll just have to accept it."

Will gives her a wry smile. "And at some point, *Christine*, you'll have to accept that *I'm* not going away either." He places his hands on the glass table. "My name is William Larson. I was born with the name. I'm pretty sure you're still Christine Casings."

His words must have pierced Christine to the core, because her face turns red, and she stalks into the house.

Will backs away from the table. "I'm going for a walk," he says over his shoulder. He glances back at me. "I'll see you later."

Mr. Larson stands and takes a few steps toward Will. They talk for a moment in hushed tones. Will's expression stays hard. He's unflinching, but Mr. Larson's face looks tortured.

Amy is pale, sick pale. She's still trying to eat, but her fingers are shaking. She lifts her chin, and our eyes catch long enough for me to see one tear trickle out of her eye and down her smooth porcelain cheek. She flashes me a quick smile. And in that moment, I see why she works so hard to stay happy and get along with everyone. The anger and conflict are unbearable. She's trying to be the one no one has to fight with. But, in the midst of it all, she's becoming invisible.

I run my fingers through my hair and try to think of something we can do that won't steal any more of our weekend. "You said your dad has a lot of movies, right?"

Amy nods.

"Why don't we clean up dinner, eat ice cream, veg out? We can each pick our favorite chick flick."

"Thanks, Ellie," she says. "That sounds perfect."

We gather our plates, load the dishwasher, and then run upstairs. I pick *Thirteen Going on Thirty* and she chooses *Ever After*, which is one of my favorites. We don't talk about the fight. We eat chocolate mint from the carton, which lowers the tension levels.

When Mr. Larson comes into the bonus room to check on us, he mentions that Will went to his friend Derek's house and might come back in the morning. Mr. Larson stands there for a while, running his hands over his face as if he needs to shave. "You girls going to be all right?"

Amy turns toward him, all sweet, "Daddy, we're fine. We're having a girls' night. Are you all right? I'm sorry Will was so mean to you and Christine."

What? Why is she blaming Will? Sure, Will was rude, but Christine was downright toxic.

Mr. Larson sits on the back of the couch and touches Amy's cheek. "Will's angry. Christine's angry. Is there ever going to be a time in my life when people aren't angry at me?"

"I'm not angry. I love you and can't wait to live with you again at the end of the summer." She pats his knee. "How's Christine?"

"She's upstairs crying, saying the whole world hates her. She'll probably go shopping tomorrow and blow off steam, or maybe she won't come out of the room for a couple of days." He runs his hands through his hair, then gets up, and leaves the room, closing the door behind him.

Amy sighs. "I wish Will would make some effort to get along with Christine."

I frown. "Why is Will the one who needs to change?"

"Oh, Ellie. You like Will, so you can't see what a jerk he is. But he's making my father miserable."

I nod and decide not to disagree. But, here's how I see it:

- Mr. Larson leaves Julie for Christine.
- Julie moves out of her house for another woman, and when she goes back to her hometown, Christine over everything, even her house, which is terrible.
- Mr. Larson essentially breaks up his family for another woman, who's at least ten years younger and gorgeous (I'll give her that).
- Will, the son, who's lost a family, is expected to be nice and stop making his father miserable. Nice.
- Not to mention Amy, the sweet daughter who's never supposed to get mad about anything. The whole thing is a big mess.

I stay up late worrying about Will. I text him a couple of times, but when he doesn't respond, I fall asleep.

everything changes

Before dawn, I stir on the couch. I'm stiff and tired. I rub my eyes, stretch, and bump into someone sitting in front of me. Startled, I open my eyes.

Will's sitting on the floor with his back to me. He turns around, puts his fingers to his lips, and points to Amy who is still sleeping. I pull out my phone, which I kept tucked close, hoping Will would text, to check the time. It's still early. I stifle a yawn. He has on a white T-shirt and the same shorts he was wearing yesterday.

He shifts slightly to rest his head beside me on the couch. I run my fingers through his hair. He moves closer. His eyes are red from crying, and his expression seems worn, almost broken. My throat tightens.

He points to the couch, indicating that he wants to lie beside me. My heart lurches, but it isn't romance that's bringing him here to me. He needs to be close to someone who's on his side.

I scoot over, and he lies down, his face near mine. He wraps his arms around my waist and breathes in my hair.

He kisses my neck. We stay as silent as the early morning. He takes a deep breath and runs his fingers over my face, staring at me the way he did on the stargazing hill.

I stop breathing. My stomach flip-flops, but then I get that everything-is-right-because-you're-here feeling.

I tremble. My eyes brim with tears. I want to tell him how much I understand his anger. I know what it's like to lose the only thing that really matters in life, but I can't talk. I can hardly breathe. I reach out and touch his cheek.

Will cradles my face in his hands. I shake my head and pull back. I stare at him for a moment. He waits, watching me think through this moment. Everything will change if we kiss.

I've been fighting these feelings all summer. I've been terrified of caring too much. I'm still terrified. I'm afraid he'll think Nadine's a better kisser than me. I'm afraid he'll think he's making a mistake. And part of me's afraid Amy is right, and Will's a player.

All these thoughts flash through my mind like a movie reel, but then I remember sitting with Will in the lighthouse, and on the beach, and how he's the only one who knows about my life, because he cared enough to wait for the answer. I think about all the days this summer we got up early and worked on the restoration. I think about how I like him. Really like him. I think about how his lips would feel on mine.

I set my hand on his chest. And then his hands are in my hair. He shifts closer. He draws my face toward him with one hand and gently places his other hand on the small of my back. His lips barely touch mine. They're soft and tender, like he's been waiting to do this since the moment we first met.

The kiss deepens, and his lips are strong and rich, and take all of me. I disappear and feel nothing but him, know nothing but his body next to mine. The raging storm inside me quiets, and I'm calm for the first time all weekend. This is where I belong.

I run my fingers up and down his arm, letting the kiss go on longer than I planned. After a few minutes, we back away. He trails a thumb down my cheek and whispers my name.

There's so much I want to say but it's hard to put into words. I lie back on the cushion, and we stare at each other for a few moments. Then I close my eyes. Will rests his head on the pillow next to me, and the tension drains from his body. I run my fingers through his hair and do my best to comfort him. We sleep.

When I rouse, Will's eyes are shut, and he's breathing steadily. Amy is sleeping on the other side of the L-shaped couch. She's hardly moved all night. I shift, hoping not to wake Will. I don't want his dad or Amy to see us on the couch together, and I don't want any more fighting. I try to slide out of his arms, but Will tightens his grip.

He doesn't open his eyes, but in a low voice, he says, "Where do you think you're going?"

His hair is messy, and his face is soft and worry-free. He looks so hot that I bite my lip to stop myself from reaching over and kissing him.

I gently slip from his encircling arms. I smooth my hair and check my watch. Almost noon. Someone's mowing a lawn outside, and in the distance kids are laughing and playing.

Will sits up and takes my hand. "Ellie?"

"Hmm?"

"Are you all right?"

I face him and whisper, "Yeah, but I don't want your dad or Christine to see us on the couch together."

Will rubs his eyes. "I don't care what they think."

"But Amy does, and I don't want to cause anymore problems for your family."

"Amy needs to get over herself. She's spineless, and I'm sick of it."

I lower my voice. "She's your sister, Will. You're different, but you can't blow her off. She cried last night, you know."

"Amy cried because she doesn't want anyone to hurt my dad's feelings." He looks at his sister for a moment. "She wasn't crying because she was worried about me. Not even for a second."

I don't want to argue with Will, and he might be right. "What are you going to do?" I ask.

"I'm going to stay at a friend's house."

Amy's voice surprises us both. "You wouldn't?" She sits up.

"Morning, Amy," Will says without looking at her.

"I can't believe how selfish you are Will," Amy tells him. "The only thing Dad cared about was if you were coming this weekend, and now you're leaving? How much longer are you going to make him suffer for trying to be happy?"

Will stands and moves me out of his way with a gentle familiarity.

Amy raises one eyebrow. "Ellie, you know I'm right, don't you? Will should stay and work it out with our dad."

I stare at the couch, rubbing the edge with my palm. "I'm not going to get involved. This is between you guys."

"Of course you take his side." Amy narrows her eyes at both of us. "You guys are together now, aren't you?" She raises her arms in exasperation. "Great, Will, one more person who'll pick you over me."

Will points a finger at his sister. "Not another word. Ellie has nothing to do with this fight. She doesn't even know the whole story, and even though I'd like her to come with me, she won't. She'll stay here with you."

I gulp. Will squeezes my shoulder, and I stare at the couch cushions as he walks away.

Amy glances over, her face full of remorse. "Sorry, Ellie. I never say the right things when I'm mad at my brother. I know we're friends, and I don't care if you two like each other."

"Thanks, Amy," is all I say.

"I'm going to take a shower, unless you want to go first?"

I shake my head. "No, that's all right. I'll clean up some of our stuff and get in the shower when you're done."

Amy leaves the bonus room. Should I go and see Will while she's gone? I'm sad that he's leaving early, and although the whole mess with his dad seems unfair, I wish he'd stay and work it out.

For the first time since my mom's death, I clearly see the root of my sadness: the finality of everything. I'll never talk to her again. About anything. I can't fix it. I can never erase those words I said with such anger. A torrent of fear and guilt whirls inside me. My body tightens, and tears threaten to tumble out. I put my hand over my mouth, forcing back a cry.

Will could fix it with his dad. He has time. At least he could try. He shouldn't destroy their relationship. I have to warn him. At least he still has a dad.

I creep out of the bonus room. The downstairs is empty. Mr. Larson must be the one mowing the lawn, and Christine's door is closed. I tiptoe to Will's door and tap on it. He opens it as he is putting a shirt on, and his pants are still partway unzipped.

I duck my head and stay in the doorway. "Sorry," I say. "I didn't mean..."

"Come in." He tugs at my hand and draws me into the room.

I step through the doorway, keeping my eyes down as he zips his shorts. I study the books on his shelves, but Will takes my hand and turns me to face him. He wraps me in his arms. He smells of fresh soap, a hint of cologne, and himself, which makes my head spin.

"Hi, there," he whispers. Taking my face in his hands, he kisses me full on the lips.

I try to hold myself together, but his nearness makes it hard to concentrate. I'm not sure what to say. Our relationship has moved to a new place, but I have no idea where that place is, and I don't want to ask. I don't want him to laugh at me or tell me that just because we kissed, it doesn't mean we're together or anything. I squirm away and sit on his bed.

I jiggle the zipper of my hoodie. "Will?" I ask. "Are you all right after everything yesterday?" I glance up, trying to catch his eye.

He turns toward his window, avoiding eye contact. "Yeah, I'm fine. This is why I didn't want to come. But my mom convinced me. I was stupid to think it would be different. This is how my dad and Christine are."

I try to think of what I need to say. I don't want to make him mad, but I need to explain why he should work things out with his dad. "I'm sorry she was so mean to you. Is she always like that?"

He gives a curt nod. "Nah, normally she's worse. She was on her best behavior because you were here."

I cringe. "Ouch. The thing is, Will, I was thinking maybe you should stay. It'd be nice if you didn't go home yet."

"Oh, you finally admit you like having me around?"

"You know I like being with you." I stare at the carpet. "But, your dad really wants to see you too."

He raises an eyebrow. I can't read the expression in his eyes.

"What?" He scrunches up his face. "Since when did you become the expert on my dad and me?" His voice has this edge to it like he's balancing on a thin rope holding his emotions in check.

"He seems to want to be with you."

"You don't even know him."

"I know, but it might be worth it to get along with your dad. He obviously loves you. Maybe you should try to work it out."

Will takes a step back and grips his desk chair. "What? I don't believe you're telling me this. You see me cry, we have one kiss, and now you're trying to fix me?"

I stand. "I'm not trying to fix you. I wouldn't do that." I go over and place a hand on his arm, but he brushes it away. "I have a different perspective is all."

"Ellie, I know nothing about your perspective. You keep your life private. Geez, you're like a locked safe. No one gets inside your head."

The blood drains from my face so fast I see double. I have to explain, but his words slapped me in the face. "My mom wasn't perfect either, and I hated her. I told you that." I shake my head in frustration. "But the thing is... now... now I'd do anything to be in her life, but it's too late. She's gone. Your dad's not."

Will takes a step towards his dresser. "What happened with your mom is terrible." His voice and his eyes show me he means what he's saying. "But, Ellie, the thing with my dad is between me and him. It's not really any of your business." He leans against the dresser and crosses his arms. "I'm not some crazy, abandoned dog." He waves toward the door. "I need to get ready to go," he says.

I've been dismissed.

I'm furious. Blind with rage. My throat is tight. My fingers are gripping the bottom of my hoodie so tightly they're white. My eyes well with tears, and I blink them out of my eyes. I hurry toward the door. "I was just trying to help."

"Ellie, do you know how many people want to help? Everyone in my life. Even the therapists. And finally, I think I've met someone who understands, someone who isn't going to force me to deal with something I don't want to face." He shakes his head. "I guess I was wrong."

I'm furious he's turning our friendship into a place where he gets to call all the shots. I stab my finger in his direction. "Maybe you're not a lost dog, but you are lost." I'm so upset I'm shaking. "You can ignore what I have to say, but you don't get to tell me what I'm allowed to say. Friendships aren't like that." I open the door. "I've kept some things about my mom to myself. But, I've said a hell of a lot more about my family than you have about yours."

Will's face is twisted with anger, sadness, frustration, and his whole body is rigid. "Just get out of my room."

"Sure thing." I step through the door but glance back. "But remember this, Will Larson. When I leave, I'm gone. You can't come back and pretend it never happened."

He stares at me as I shut the door.

My heart is racing so fast it feels like it's going to jump out of my body. I rush to Amy's room, undress, fling my clothes around, and jump in the shower. I stand under the running water, my back against the tile of the shower, and let warm tears roll down my cheeks.

Of course, I finally got something good, but because I just had to try to help him, it blew up, and I lost it all. Why can't I just keep my mouth shut? Why couldn't I pretend I didn't care? And why did he have to be such a jerk? My stomach aches. I run my hands over my dripping hair and force myself to stop crying.

After I get out of the shower, I stay in Amy's room to braid my hair. She's downstairs talking to her dad. Then the doorbell rings.

Will walks down the hall and past Amy's door without even a glance toward me. It happened so fast. All the build-up. Everything. It's over. He was the one good thing on that island besides Aunt Violet and the family. With him, I was real and alive.

I need to get out of the house. I shove my clothes in my bag, pick up my phone, and punch in a number.

"Ellie?" Jose's voice comes through the phone. His familiar voice calms me.

"Yeah, it's me." I sigh.

"Where are you?"

"Seattle... I was sort of hoping you could pick me up?" I press my fingers against my eyelids to hold back the tears.

He must hear the crack in my voice because he doesn't ask anything except "What's the address?"

I tell him.

"Think they'll let me into that neighborhood?" He chuckles.

"Just tell them you're the landscaper."

"Funny." He pauses. "I'll be there as soon as I can."

Amy comes into the bedroom right as I say, "Just hurry, please."

Her face gets pale. She blinks a few times. "Are you leaving too?"

"Um, I just want to hang out with a friend. He's coming to pick me up."

"You and Will had a fight, didn't you?"

She might let me go without taking it too hard if I tell her the truth. "Yes." I sigh. "Listen, it's nothing personal, but I need to get some air."

"What about the shopping?"

"Amy, I'm sorry. I don't think I'd be a fun person to be around right now. When we get back to the island, we'll hang out again. My fight with Will won't get in the way of our friendship. I promise."

"Sure," she says.

I get the feeling she's gone through this before.

Before Jose arrives, I take my bag and go down for a cup of coffee and a piece of toast.

While I'm at the table, Mr. Larson comes into the kitchen. He takes a mug from the cupboard, trying to act nonchalant, but I can tell he's dying to talk. "Amy tells me you and Will are pretty close?"

"We aren't that close. We've talked some this summer. That's it."

"Oh." His voice falls. "I thought there was more to your friendship by the way he acted around you. I must have misunderstood. The thing is, I wish someone could get through to him. The truth is, Ellie, I screwed up. I blew it." He rubs the stubble on his chin with one hand. "But, I love my kids, and it makes me sick to think Will won't forgive me. I know I hurt their mother, but I'd do anything to make things right with Will."

I wrap my hand around the coffee mug and force myself to look at him. "I hope you two work it out, Mr. Larson, I really do."

Just then, the doorbell rings. Before he leaves to open the front door, he waits a second. "Maybe you could say something to him?" He raises his eyebrows a bit.

"I don't think so, Mr. Larson. But, I hope you and Will figure out how to make the best of it."

"So do I, Ellie. So do I."

He opens the door, and Jose is there.

Gratitude overwhelms me. It's been a long time since I've seen him. But it's Jose, and he's here. I breathe a sigh of relief, and before I know it, I'm out the door.

back to the island

Before Jose opens his truck door for me, he cups my face in his hands. *"Que bueno verte."*

"It's good to see you too."

I let him enfold me in an embrace. He squeezes me hard as if he knows I need to feel safe.

I press my face against his shirt. "It's good to be seen."

"You want to talk about it?"

"Not really." I move some wisps of hair out of my eyes. "But thanks for coming. I know it was hard to get out of work."

"No problem, but now what do you want to do?" Jose gets in the car and backs out of the driveway.

"Can you take me back to the island?"

A few months ago, Orcas was the last place on earth I wanted to go to. Now, I ache for it. I want to be in my lighthouse and pretend the rest of the world is gone.

Jose turns onto the main road. "Are you sure you don't want to come home for the rest of the weekend?"

"I don't even know where home is anymore, Jose. I'm

starting to like Orcas. Sometimes it feels more like home than anywhere else I've been, but other times it feels like some weird country where I don't belong."

"I feel that way about Mexico," he says. "Torn between two worlds. At the end of the day, you gotta pick one though. You can't live in limbo forever."

"Which one do I pick?" I ask, realizing how right he is. The trailer park and Orcas are two different worlds and, ultimately, I can't have both.

"The one that is more true."

"Which one is that?"

"You'll know when you need to. Remember when I went to Mexico two summers ago? I was thinking of staying down there. My *abuela* is there and my aunts and cousins." He glances at me. "But when the summer was over, even though everyone begged me to stay, I wanted to come back here. You'll know if you want to be with your aunt and cousins – or if you want to be here."

I rest my head against the seat. What should I do? I try to forget about Will, but I can't. I want to know how he's doing. If my relationship with Will were fine, I'd probably want to stay on Orcas. But, I can't pick Orcas for a boyfriend. I have to pick Orcas because it's where I belong.

We're quiet on the drive. I snuggle close to Jose, and he wraps his arm around me. I rest my head on his shoulder and close my eyes.

Jose finds a drive-thru coffee stand before we get to the ferry line and orders me a vanilla latte. I wish I could enjoy it more, but my stomach hurts.

Maybe Amy is right. Will's a player, and I got played.

We sit inside the truck for the ferry ride. Jose runs his hand over my hair and drinks his latte. He kisses the top of my head every once in a while. I grip his hand and refuse to let go.

Once we drive off the ferry, I direct him where to go, which roads to turn on. He rolls down his window, and the warm sea air calms my jittery nerves. In the distance, seagulls squawk and dive for their next meal. The warm rays of the afternoon sun overhead shine through the window. Jose's glancing around, taking in his surroundings. We drive along Main Street past Julie's Café. I put Will out of my mind, but my head feels cramped, as if I've shoved too many thoughts and emotions into the corners, and they're going to start leaking out.

When Jose pulls into the driveway, he gasps. "This is where your mom grew up?" His mouth hangs open.

I nod. "Violet and Ben remodeled it after they got married, but, yeah, my mom grew up here."

Jose's silence is striking. The contrast between this and the rundown trailer park we've lived in our whole lives is overwhelming. It's not like the farmhouse is all that amazing. It's that it's permanent. It's a home. There's something very transient about a trailer.

"Are you going to introduce me to everyone?" He opens the truck door.

I nod and smile.

He pulls my bag from the bed of the truck.

Violet is barbecuing chicken on the grill and batting at the smoke with her metal tongs. She's wearing her pink apron, and her hair is fixed in two braids like a little girl. My guess is Prissy's been playing hair parlor.

The smell of barbecued chicken makes my stomach growl. The picnic table's set with potato salad, baked beans, and watermelon. Violet spies me through the barbecue smoke and smiles her big I'm-so-happy-to-see-you smile, which makes something almost hurt deep inside me.

I wave. "Hi, Violet."

"Hey there, girl," Violet says. Then she squints at Jose.

"You remember Jose, right?" I ask.

Violet smiles at him. "I do. It's good to see you again, Jose." Then she pinches her lips together, like she's trying to figure out what to say. "Ellie, is everything all right?"

"Yeah. I wanted to come back early, and Jose picked me up."

"Can you stay for dinner, Jose? We have plenty."

Jose nods. "Can we help you?" He reaches for a tray of chicken.

"Sure. But be careful. This smoke might torch your lungs."

"What's the occasion?" I eye the picnic table.

"Too hot inside. But since you're back, we'll say you're the occasion. We missed you." Violet touches my shoulder, kisses my cheek and then wraps me into a bear hug. My ribs actually hurt. She pats my cheek and stares hard into my eyes as if she's trying to figure out if I'm all right. I pat her on the back a couple of times.

"The kitchen is hot enough to fry eggs on the floor," she says. "I couldn't bear to cook inside. So I told Ben, 'We're gonna have us a picnic.'" She hands me a platter, fills it with hot chicken, and loads another platter with corn on the cob.

Then we all head for the table.

"So, how are Ken and Christine?" Violet asks as we sit down. "How'd everything go?" She motions the kids over.

"Will left early too." I dish a spoonful of potato salad onto my plate, trying to pretend it isn't a big deal.

"Julie told me. Amy called to say she's not coming back for a few more days. Her dad'll take her to the ferry sometime this week. Julie wondered if Will had done anything to hurt you. Everything all right between you two?"

"Everything's fine."

Violet squints at me like she's trying to decide if she believes me or not. "I'll let her know." Her voice sounds unconvinced.

I take a bite of potato salad, hoping Violet will drop the conversation. I don't want to talk about Will in front of Jose.

Later Jose and I drive into town, and I show him

the shops. We buy coffee at Julie's Café and walk to the bookstore. Being inside reminds me of the first time I saw Will sitting on the chair reading his book like he owned the store. I pull out my phone. Nothing. *What a jerk.*

Will tells me he likes me, breaks up with Nadine and everything, but at the first sign of trouble, he bolts. I can't believe I let myself fall for him.

After a while Jose drops me back at the house so he can catch the evening ferry. I wish he could stay the night, but he has to work.

When I'm getting out of the car, Jose stops me. "Ellie?" He takes my hand and doesn't lift his eyes. He clears his throat. "It's a guy, isn't it?"

I nod. "Yeah. But it's over."

"In all the years I've known you, I've never seen you care this much about a guy. Not even me."

"That's not true, Jose."

"Yes, it is. I can see it in your face. You like him."

"Whatever it was, it's over now."

"I doubt that," he says. "Don't be too proud to admit you need someone, Ellie. You don't have to do everything by yourself."

I open my mouth to talk, but he interrupts.

"Ellie, I want to say something about this island."

"OK..."

Jose rests his hands on the steering wheel. "Whatever you decide to do in a few weeks is fine. If you want to come and stay with us, that's great, because we miss you like crazy. But I can tell they really love you here."

When I start to speak, Jose holds up his hand. "Let me finish. The reason I go to Mexico every few summers isn't because I like to drink tequila and party with my cousins. Well, maybe a little." He grins. "But it's mostly because I'm trying to remember where I came from. All that crap about roots and stuff – there's a lot of truth to it. I come back though, because Mexico doesn't have anything for me in the long term."

He gestures toward the white farmhouse. "I don't think it's the same for you. No matter what you think, Ellie, it wasn't your fault. The whole thing with your mom was messed up from beginning to end. There's wasn't anything you could do. And when you accept that, you'll see this island has a lot for you."

I close my eyes. Jose takes my hand.

"You really don't think it was my fault?" My voice is so soft I can barely hear it, and it wobbles, threatening to take me over an emotional edge.

Jose cups my cheek and leans his forehead against mine. "I wish I could make it better for you."

A tear escapes and slides down my cheek. I duck my head to hide it and open the door.

Jose reaches for my hand. "Let me know if I need to come over here and beat that guy up."

"Thank you for picking me up and for... for everything. I miss you." I jump to the ground and slam the door.

"Anything for you, Ellie. Anything."

I trace the outline of his truck as it goes down the driveway and disappears from sight. I'm emptier than before. Jose's words burn inside of me. Everything has changed. I can't pretend I belong in the trailer park anymore.

I tiptoe into the kitchen, assuming everyone is asleep. I jump when Violet asks, "Jose leave?"

Violet's at the table reading a book and drinking a cup of tea.

"Yeah. He has to work tomorrow."

"He cares for you."

It's hard to explain the depth of our relationship to people. There's such a deep bond. "Yeah, we've been through a lot together."

She grips her teacup. "You must really miss him."

I stand up straighter. "I do."

"Too bad he couldn't stay a little longer."

"He has to work in the morning, but it meant a lot that he dropped everything to pick me up." I've probably just said too much. That was like an open invitation for Violet to ask about Will.

"I'm glad Jose came. Julie mentioned there was a family fight with Will in the middle of it. I'm sorry you had to deal with that."

I shrug, but my palms heat, and my face feels hotter. "Yeah, I just needed to get away." I try to make my voice confident and neutral, but it's cloaked in emotions that betray me.

"I can imagine you wanted to get away. It must have been hard to see Will fight with his dad. I hope everything's OK between you now, and with Amy?"

"I'm hoping Amy will get over it. As for Will, we're not friends anymore." That thought makes my heart hurt. I put my hand to put temple. I have to go to bed.

"I'm sorry, Ellie." She stands up. "I'm sure he'll come around. I hope it's not too late when he does. I think he needs a friend like you."

I run both hands over my head to smooth out my hair. Without even thinking about it, a different question tumbles out of me. "Violet, why did you say it must have been hard to see him fighting?"

Violet picks up her teacup, walks to the sink and puts it in, then rests her back against the counter. "I can only imagine you're struggling with regret over how you wish things could have been with your mom. To see Will fighting with his dad has to be hard. The thing is, Ellie, your mom was sad most of your life. Unfortunately, you were born into that sadness – nothing you could have done to stop it."

I gulp. It's hard to talk. "How come you haven't asked me about anything?"

"You weren't ready. Most people say what they think

you want to hear. If I asked when you got here, you wouldn't have told me. You'll talk when you're ready."

"That's OK with you?"

"Of course it's OK. Ellie. I love you. And whatever it is you feel guilty about, it's not as bad as you think."

My eyes well with tears. I stare at my feet. "You don't know that," I whisper. It's much worse.

"Maybe not, but I do know you're not the only person who's ever felt guilty."

I'm sure that's true, but there's a difference between false guilt and the real thing. Mine is there for a reason. I'm to blame.

questions and answers

I wake the next morning with a burning ache to see my lighthouse. I glance at my phone before getting out of bed. Nothing. It really is over with Will.

I'm going to check on Maggie, and I'm desperate to sit by the lighthouse and stare at the sea. My heart hurts, actually hurts. I can't eat. I didn't slept well.

Should I call Will? No. I refuse to become one of those girls who emails and calls twenty times a day until he finally gives in and talks. Besides, if I can't be honest with a friend, who can I be honest with? I need to accept he's gone. My eyes well with tears, but I brush them away. I won't cry. I got used to disappointment and loss a long time ago.

I climb down the trail to see about Maggie. She growls when I get close, but that's all.

I fill her dish and sit in the dirt, staring at her cave. "Maggie, I'm not going to hurt you. I want you to trust me. Why won't you let me help you?"

Her shadow wavers back and forth in the darkness

of the cave. The pups are wiggling, whimpering. Maggie trots out and stares at me.

"I fought with Will. That's why he's not here." I hug my knees tightly, wanting to feel protected. "He's mad at his dad, and that scared me. Really scared me. I was angry with mom, and she died. She's gone, and I can't take it back." I rest my chin against my knees. Now Will's mad at me. The thing is, I like him. I even liked who I was when we were together."

Maggie's still lying at the edge of the cave staring at me as though listening to every word. I inch closer.

She growls.

"Sorry, Maggie, I won't push it, but I'd like to be your friend." I stand, brush the dirt off my pants, and climb the cliff, even though the very thought of going into the lighthouse without Will makes me choke up. I walk with my head down, my eyes on the trail.

As I near the cottage door, the old man's voice comes from behind me. "I thought I made it clear that this isn't your lighthouse."

I jump and turn. He's three feet away, off to one side. His skin is wrinkled, pale like chalk dust, and he's propped up by his cane.

His territorial attitude tips me over the emotional edge. "Whose lighthouse is it then?" I stand up straighter. The anger in my voice takes me by surprise.

"Rose's lighthouse," he says.

"You've said that before, but I don't see anybody named Rose around here. Where is she, if this is her lighthouse?"

He turns around and back again, his eyes searching, as if for some sign of Rose's whereabouts. Then he scratches his head. "I don't know where Rose is. She's been gone a long time. I'm waiting for her to come back. I need to make it right, to tell her I'm sorry."

"For what?"

"Why do you care?" He juts out his chin.

"Just asking is all."

"I lied to her." He squints. "Who are you, anyway?"

"My name is Ellie. What's yours?"

"Henry." He glances around again as if expecting her to appear. "I miss Rose."

My eyes get misty. "I miss Rose too."

"You know Rose?"

"I did." My voice sounds hollow. "She died a few months ago."

"She died? Rose isn't dead. She's got to come back. I need her to come to this lighthouse. I've got something to tell her."

A lone tear drips down my face. I blink a couple of times. "The Rose I knew is gone. She's not coming back." I point to the lighthouse door. "Do you mind if I go in, Henry?"

"Maybe Rose won't mind. She's coming back. One day, she'll return and forgive me for what I did."

My skin prickles. I reach for the doorknob, still watching him, but then pause. "What did you do, Henry?"

"I can't tell you. But if you see Rose, tell her I need to talk to her. I gotta make things right." He takes a few steps into the wood.

I turn my eyes for a moment to get the key into the lock, and when I turn back, he's vanished. There's a chill in the air. I shiver and rub my arms. *Who is he? Am I seeing ghosts?* But Will saw him too.

I go inside the cottage, hoping to sit down for a while and think, be quiet. But once I'm there, I see Will in every empty space, and it's more than I can handle. I run home.

I dash up the front porch steps. Prissy is rocking back and forth on the swing, and Violet is kneeling in the garden pulling weeds. The twins are playing in their sandbox nearby.

Prissy sees me and smiles. "Where've you been, Ellie? Everyone's looking for you."

"What do you mean?" I sit beside her on the swing.

Prissy sets her hand on my leg.

Aunt Violet straightens from her crouched position "Amy called, so did Alex and Jake. They all want you to call them back. They wondered why you didn't answer your phone."

I nod. "Thanks. Do you want me to help with lunch or anything?"

"No, Ben said he'd get it ready in a few minutes. Thanks, though."

"I'm going to find something to read."

"Aren't you going to call your friends?" Prissy asks.

"Not today."

I spend the rest of the day trying to read a novel, but I can't. I'm filled with too many thoughts. Will, the old man named Henry, my mom. The pain that threatened to take me out a few months ago is now an ache taking over my heart. I want my mom.

I'm upstairs on my window seat studying the landscape around me. Everything in me wants to call Will and tell him about Henry, what he said, but I won't.

Finally, I decide to look through the jumble on the bookshelves for the family albums.

Maybe I'll find out more about my mom. I'd like to see if Violet has any pictures of Henry. The albums are in a bookcase on the second floor landing. I sit at the foot of the stairs leading to my room and page through them.

Violet is one of the most disorganized people I've ever met, and her albums are true to form: no rhyme or reason to any of them. I'll have to put them in order to find anything.

I leaf through every book she has. Pictures of the twins and Prissy, of her wedding, and of Ben working on the farmhouse renovations are numerous. Each picture makes me more and more thankful I came here and a little more left out. I finally find pictures of my mom in high school, laughing and running, swimming, riding horses with her friends. Almost always with Violet. I can't breathe. I trace the outline of her face with my thumb. She's beautiful. Her blond hair shines, her skin looks vibrant. Her smile's contagious, like Violet said. She's not the same woman I lived with my whole life.

I don't find anything that gives me any clue my mom knew Henry or someone who looked like Henry.

I'm sitting cross-legged, pictures strewn around me, when Violet steps out of her bedroom holding a shoe-sized box.

"Ellie?" Violet stops in the doorway.

"Yeah?" I'm so engrossed in the albums, I barely turn.

"I found this box a few months ago. I'm not sure what's inside. I thought you should be the first one to look through it. It was an important box to your mom." She hands it to me.

"Thanks, Violet." I take it from her, then climb upstairs. I sit on my window seat, take a deep breath, and ease open the box.

Inside, I find an album, a few loose pictures, and some keepsakes like track ribbons and a 4-H ribbon. I flip open the picture album. The first picture is of the lighthouse. My mom's standing at the door with a gorgeous smile on her face, glowing with happiness. I choke up, put my hand to my mouth. I can't breathe for a second. My hand trembles. She was beautiful. So full of life.

I go through the pictures of her parents, Violet, and some friends. I recognize Julie and Mr. Larson, which is weird. At the back of the album are two pictures that bring a lump to my throat.

They hold the answers, or at least traces of the answers, I'm looking for. I recognize Henry almost immediately. He's much younger, less wrinkled, and his face is hopeful, with no sign of the despair I see every time he appears at the lighthouse. He has brown hair and dark eyes. He's standing at the helm of an old ship in the blazing sun. Could he be my father?

I turn to the other picture and gasp. A man stands on

the beach below the lighthouse. He looks like me, or I look like him. The dark eyes and hair, the shape of his face. His dark skin sends shivers down my back. He must be my father. My hand trembles. I rub my arms, pulling my legs up close to myself. I have a father, somewhere. Or I did.

I study the outline of his face, then clutch the picture to my chest. I have to talk to Violet. I need some answers. I hope her answers will bring my heart and mind some relief. I ache to know it wasn't my fault, or at least not all my fault.

I want what Henry wants – forgiveness. The problem is that the only one who can forgive me is dead.

Violet's story

The next morning I wake early, before anyone else, and dress in a hurry. I whistle for Goldie who's grazing among the trees in the orchard. She nuzzles me and almost pushes me over. I mount, give her a firm squeeze, and she gallops all the way to the lighthouse. The trail is bone dry. Dust billows around my feet as I find my stride. The warm salt air calms my nervous stomach. Water swishes softly against the rocky cliff up ahead.

First, to Maggie's cave. I have a dog treat to give her. I kneel in the dirt as close as I dare. "MAAAGIEEE," I call.

She peers out of the cave.

"Hey, girl." I wait for a second. "I have a treat." I hold it out and wait. I wait so long my arm gets tired.

She finally takes a few steps toward me. I stay stone still. She comes one step closer. Then one more. She stretches her neck and grabs the treat. Then she darts back into her cave.

"Good girl," I tell her. "I knew you could do it. I'll be back with more." I wish Will could have seen that.

I squint and peer over, trying to see the pups. Three of them are crawling around, whimpering.

When I climb the ridge to the lighthouse, Henry appears out of nowhere. He's hunched over his cane, beside Goldie, who must see him, but is acting rather indifferent. He's more shriveled, and his face is pale.

"Hey, Henry." *Am I talking a ghost or a crazy old man?*

He glances around. "You weren't trying to help that dog again were you?"

"Why are you so against me helping her?" I ask.

"She's crazy."

"She had puppies. I want to help the pups."

"You'll have to kill her to get those pups from her."

"She came closer to me today than she's ever come."

"You probably had food. That doesn't mean she's safe now. It means she's hungry." He shifts his weight on his cane. "You seen Rose here today? Feels like she's near."

I bite my lip. "No, I haven't seen Rose, but I want to ask you about her." It hurts my throat to say my mom's name.

"What do you want to know?" He faces the sea.

"I was wondering if you'd tell me what you lied about."

Henry flips his hand. "Why should I tell you?" There's a tinge of accusation is his voice.

I glance out at the water. "Sometimes it helps to tell the truth."

He leans in as though he wants to make sure no one can overhear. "I lied. I was jealous. My plan hurt her." His eyes fill with deep sorrow.

"What plan? What did you do?"

He points to the lighthouse. "He was going to take her away from me," he cries out and buries his face in his hands.

The cry comes from deep inside him and sends a prickle down my spine.

"Why'd you leave, Rose? Why did you have to go?" He

hurries into the woods, disappearing once again.

I can't breathe. I have to piece this together. Even though I'm more afraid of hearing the truth than anything before in my whole life, I have to hear what Violet has to say. It doesn't matter that I'm so afraid I can hardly breathe. It's time to find out the truth. And once I hear Violet's story, maybe I'll have the courage to tell someone mine.

Violet's pouring coffee into her mug when I walk in. She glances at me with those eyes that make me think she's been waiting. I run past her and lunge up the stairs two steps at a time and then race up the next flight to the attic. I grab the two pictures and run back downstairs. I hand Violet the pictures.

"I'm ready to hear who these men are."

Violet runs her thumb across Henry's face.

"Ellie, I'll be right back." She sets her mug on the counter. "I have to get something in my room. I'll meet you on the front porch."

When she comes down a few minutes later, she takes my arm and tucks it into hers. "It's strange," she says. "Somehow I knew it was time to tell you." She tips her head to the sky and sighs.

Then arm in arm, we take the path that leads to the lighthouse.

"Rose and I were eighteen months apart. For most of our lives, we did everything together. She was the beautiful sister and could make anyone, and I mean anyone, laugh. She had the kind of laugh that made everything feel good inside."

That laugh never made it off this island.

Violet points behind her toward the house. "We grew up in the same farmhouse where we live now, except it was rundown and ugly.

"My dad was an alcoholic and struggled to keep a job. My mom worked hard holding everything together. She told me and Rose, almost daily, that she didn't marry for love; she married out of necessity. I think she loved us girls, but life was hard. It seemed like we were always trudging up a hill, but never got to run down it.

"Finally, when I was eighteen and Rose was seventeen, Mom died of breast cancer. She'd suffered for years, and my dad didn't do anything to help her. That's when Rose took to going to the lighthouse."

I never heard a word about my grandmother. Every time I asked my mom about family she changed the subject.

"After Mom died, my dad drank even more. He let the farm go. Rose and I did our best to hold everything together, but she hated it. She had dreams of getting off the island, but there didn't seem to be any way of escape. And she missed our mother."

Violet squeezes my arm. "I know what it's like to miss your mom, Ellie. I remember it."

I can't talk. My whole body seems paralyzed. Caught between racing thoughts and fearful ones.

"Rose was probably the most popular girl on the island. One boy in particular loved her his whole life. Henry. He's in one of the pictures you have. The one on the ship."

The same Henry who comes to the lighthouse? But he's so old.

Violet continues, "They didn't hang out a lot, but everyone knew how much he loved her. Rose liked the attention, and over time, came to depend on Henry's affection. He loved her so much it hurt to watch him, but Rose didn't love him back."

"What did Henry do?" My voice is quiet, hoarse. I hardly recognize it.

"He was a fisherman. At the time, fishing in Alaska was good money, and Henry became wealthy. He saved everything, hoping even if Rose didn't love him, she might at least marry him for his money. She almost did.

"Then our dad was driving drunk one night and drove into a tree. His death made us feel even more alone and lost than before. And Rose took to hanging out by the lighthouse all the time."

No wonder I'm drawn to the lighthouse.

"One summer day Rose was waitressing at the local pub when a group of young guys from the University of Washington showed up. They were summer interns, doing a study on Orca whales. One of the guys, Alejandro Ramirez, liked your mom. Especially her long blonde hair. They flirted for a few days and went out a few times. I saw something come alive in her."

I'm hanging in suspense. Every word makes me more desperate. *Is he my father?*

"He came from Chile. They made plans for her to fly down to Chile and meet his family. Rose really thought it might work out with them."

She stops in the road and turns to me. "The thing is, Ellie, he never came back."

"What do you mean?"

"She waited and waited. Then Henry came to our house and explained he'd seen Alejandro on the ferry. Alejandro told him that he was already engaged to some other woman in Chile, and even though he really liked your mom, he couldn't see her again. Henry had agreed to break the news."

Oh my God. That's what he lied about.

Violet keeps talking. I try to focus. "That betrayal hurt her in a way I can't really explain, Ellie. I figured out she was pregnant before she did. All the while, Henry waited. She almost married him when she realized she was going to have a baby, but right before the wedding, she ran away to Seattle.

"Your mom couldn't put Henry through a loveless marriage. She packed her bags and left. Pregnant and with no money, no education, no parents to help her out, and struggling with a broken heart. I begged your mom to stay here, and I also begged to go with her. She wanted neither."

"I didn't hear anything until the day you were born, Eleanor." She holds out a worn piece of paper. "I saved the letter she wrote from the hospital. I didn't put it in the box, because I wanted to read it to you."

Violet finds a patch of grass on the side of the path and sits down. I sit beside her, desperate to hear, yet terrified at the same time.

I recognize my mom's handwriting. She always wrote quickly, like chicken scratch.

Dear Violet,

It's a girl. I named her Eleanor Marianne Martinson. She looks like Alejandro. I thought that would make me sad, but it doesn't. I just love that she's mine.

I'll do my best to take care of her. I don't have a lot to give her, but I'll give her all I have.

Rose

I put my hand over my mouth to keep from crying, but the tears keep coming like someone opened a dam and released the pent-up water. I reach out for the letter with a trembling hand. All these years, I was convinced she didn't love me. But she did. I thought it was me – and the truth is – it wasn't. She wanted me. She was glad I was hers.

This is so much worse. It makes my words a hundred times worse.

It takes me moments or hours. I'm not sure, but finally I string some words together. "Violet?" I ask when I can form a clear thought. "Whatever happened to Henry?"

Violet picks up a bit of dirt and lets it slide to the ground. "Interesting you should ask," she says. "Henry went crazy. He went off on his ship and kept fishing, but became crazier and crazier every time we saw him. He came into port around the time I went to get you. When Ben saw him, he told Henry your mom had died. Ben said Henry looked pretty hopeless."

I tighten my hands into fists and start breathing faster.

"Later that day, he fell off one of the cliffs by the lighthouse."

I jerk back like someone splashed ice water in my face. "He died?"

"Almost. He hit his head and is in a coma. He has brain activity, but hasn't woken up. Such a tragedy. They didn't fly him to the city hospital. He's at the tiny hospital in town."

I'm shaking. I am seeing ghosts. Or at least, I'm seeing some freaky part of some man who lied to my mother.

"Ellie?" Violet reaches over, squeezes one of my shaking hands. She stands brushes the dirt off her shorts. "I think we should walk home. I'll get you some breakfast. You need to eat something."

"Maybe you're right." I stand. It's unbearable. It's worse than I ever could have imagined. And to top it off, I'm having some sort of weird soulful experience with a man who is actually in a coma.

Henry's Story

When we walk into the house Ben is at the kitchen sink doing the breakfast dishes. "Ellie, you're mighty popular, aren't you?" He wipes and rinses a plate. "Amy called again. Jake and Alex called. Oh, and Will just called."

My head jerks up at Will's name.

Ben smiles. "Will, in particular, seemed eager for you to call him back. I told them to call your cell, but they said they'd tried several times and got no answer."

I don't say anything. I'm not up for an argument, and I don't have it in me to hear Will say anything else that could hurt me. I'm so fragile, it scares me. I don't want to be weak, but I am. And alone.

Violet puts toast in the toaster, pours orange juice, and seats me at the kitchen table. She must sense I need something normal to occupy my time. After I take a few bites of toast, the phone rings.

Violet answers it. She gives me a look.

I wave my hand in the air. I don't want to talk to anyone. I'm too raw to put coherent words together.

"It's Amy," Violet whispers.

Since Amy's called a bunch of times in the last two days, I should probably talk to her.

"Hello," I say.

"For goodness' sake, Ellie, where in the world have you been? It's like you fell into the rabbit hole, and now you're gone forever. And what is going on between you and my brother? He keeps asking about you."

"Hi, Amy." I move into the hallway. "I've been right here. No rabbit hole for me."

"Is that all you're going to say? Ellie? Did you hear me? I asked what happened with you and my brother?"

"Nothing. Anyway, nothing was going on between your brother and me in the first place."

"Ellie, sometimes you're so frustrating. We're friends, aren't we?"

The last thing I want right now is some girl issue with Amy. "Sure we're friends. The thing with Will's not a big deal. Like I said, it never really started."

Amy barely pauses. "He's acting like the world has fallen apart, and my brother never does that. And all you say is that it's no big deal? Well, he sure isn't acting as calm as you."

What do I tell her? It's hard to believe Will is that upset. "I think it's better if I just leave this one alone."

"Really? Most girls in Will's life call him like a hundred times a day. And you? Not even once. Whatever. But I'm not going to be your go-between."

"I don't need a go-between. Don't worry."

"Jake is having an end of the summer party tomorrow night at his house. Can you come?"

"I'm not sure. I need to ask Violet and Ben."

"Yeah, yeah, yeah. We both know they'll say yes. Just say you'll come."

"I'll try, Amy. I have to go."

After I hang up, Violet raises an eyebrow. "You want to tell me what's going on with you and Will?"

"I don't want to talk about it."

"Maybe he wants to apologize," Violet says, ignoring the fact that I don't want to talk about it.

"Maybe, but what happens afterward? I mean, what if I say the wrong thing tomorrow, and he yells at me again? I can't be friends with someone who decides all the rules."

"Maybe you should tell him that. I doubt Will is accustomed to being friends with someone who won't let him make all the rules. He's pretty determined."

"I know. He's the one who wanted to hang out and be friends, then when I say one thing about how he should give his dad a chance, he yells at me."

"That's what you're fighting about?" Violet sets her toast on her plate.

"His dad might have made some bad decisions, but he's still his dad, isn't he? That's all I tried to say."

My aunt's eyes fill up with tears. "Eleanor, you are one of the most special girls I have ever known." She steps over and hugs me, embracing me for a long time. "I wish I could help you see how beautiful you are." She runs her hand over my hair.

I stare at the table. It's still awkward when she hugs me. "Thanks, Violet." My voice cracks. She doesn't know the truth. If she knew, she wouldn't say those things.

"Try to talk to him." She releases me. "From what I've seen, Will's pretty honest. If he's trying to get a hold of you, he wants to make it right."

I shrug. "I'll think about it." I start to head upstairs but turn back to Aunt Violet. There's still something I want to know. "Do you think my mom loved Alejandro all these years?"

She runs a finger around the rim of her coffee cup. "I don't know. From the little you've told me and the things I've tried to piece together, I don't think your mom ever figured out how to stand on her own two feet. The heartbreak and pain of everything kept moving her in a direction against life, not for it. I do know this – your mom loved you. No matter what happened at the end, Rose loved you."

I nod, but the guilt sits in my stomach. I can't hold it together anymore. I hate what I did to my mom. If I hadn't been so angry with her, it would all be different. Somehow I need to find a way to tell the truth, to get it out.

Maybe if I talk to Henry and find out exactly what he lied about, it'll help me piece everything together.

"I'm going to the lighthouse."

"Sure, Ellie, but I think you should go to that party tomorrow night. It's important you stay connected with your other friends, even if you and Will are having problems."

I'm not in the mood to argue and she means well. "Sure."

I don't stop to see Maggie. I run right past the trail and toward the lighthouse. I stand by the door, hoping Henry will come.

He says he lied to her. Did he lie about Alejandro? How do I get some guy's soul to tell me the truth?

He keeps coming to the lighthouse for a reason, though. Maybe he wants to tell me.

When he appears, he's hunched over his cane, and his breathing is forced – like it pains him to inhale.

"Henry."

His eyes are clouded over. "I'm tired," he says. "So tired." He takes another breath, and his chest rattles.

I step out of the doorway. "Will you tell me what you lied to Rose about?"

He coughs, leaning hard on his cane. He glances to his right and to his left, as if to make sure no one sees him. "Why do you want to know?"

"It might help me."

"Promise you won't tell Rose? I need to tell her myself."

"I promise."

He shifts his weight from one foot to the other. "That man from Chile. I hated him. He came here thinking he was great. Thinking he could just take what he wanted. I stood by waiting, hoping he'd leave, but they started making plans." He shakes his head, like he still can't believe it.

The blood drains from my face.

"He told everyone he loved her. That he wanted to take her to Chile and marry her. I couldn't let that happen. She was mine. I'd loved her too long." Henry coughs, breathes in one of his raspy breaths. "I told her he was gonna marry someone else. I told him Rose and I were getting married. It was all a lie."

I stare at him. Not sure I heard right. "The man from Chile wasn't going to marry someone else?"

"No. I told him Rose didn't want to end it herself, so she sent me to end it for her. But the truth is that she loved him. He left her a letter even. I never gave it to her."

My hands tremble, and then my whole body starts shaking. Alejndro loved her. Henry tricked my mom. He ruined my life. Everything flashes before my eyes. My whole world could have been different. It could have been happy. I could have had a happy ending. Oh. My. God.

A bird squawks in the distance, and the wind shifts just enough that the smell of salt water surrounds me. "What did you do with the letter?"

"I put it in the lighthouse. In the bookcase."

I pull the key out of my pocket. My hand shakes as I turn it in the hole. I shove open the door and rush to the bookcase.

He stumbles through the doorway. "It's inside *Jane Eyre*. She always liked that book."

Why? Why am I finding this out now? Why couldn't

this have happened when my mom was still here? Pain. The shame swirls in my heart, and I'm caught in the undertow. The hurt, the horror drags me down like an anchor in my heart. I lived my whole life in a trailer park with a broken woman all because another man was jealous. Henry stole my life.

I open *Jane Eyre*, my favorite book, and the note is there with my mom's name on the worn piece of paper.

Anger boils up inside me. "You lied to them?" I wave the letter in his wrinkled face. "What gave you the right to lie?" My voice gets louder and louder. I hear myself screaming. "You ruined her life!"

He hangs his head, and the pain in his eyes is almost unbearable. I can't look at him.

"I have to tell her the truth," he says. "I shouldn't have done it."

I clench my hand into a fist and open it quickly, hitting my palm against the wall. "You can't tell Rose anything. She's dead." I turn to him, and rage explodes from me. "She killed herself six months ago." My voice chokes. The words fell like stones.

He stumbles backward and gasps. "No! Not my Rose. She can't be dead. You're a liar. She's coming back to her lighthouse, and I'll make it right." He presses a hand to his forehead, covering his eyes.

Without intending to, I drop *Jane Eyre*. It bangs onto the ground. "You can't, Henry. It's too late." I stop. *It is too late.* Too late for him. It's too late for me. And it's too late for my mom. My own guilt is haunting me just like Henry's. We share the same despair. The despair of the guilt-ridden.

He hobbles off into the woods and vanishes.

Time stops. I stare out at the water, my shattered life lying in pieces all around me. I can't pick them up. Everything's too broken.

When I can almost breathe again, someone steps into the light. I gasp. It's Will.

"Ellie?" Will sounds worried.

I'm still too startled to say anything. I'm staring at the ground. My heart is battered. I can't talk to Will right now.

"I came to talk to you. I heard you yelling at the old man. What's going on?"

His voice is calm, and it settles me. His words bring me back to the present. He takes a step closer and touches my arm. I brush away his hand and step back.

"What's going on Will?" I ask.

"I want to talk to you." He comes closer. "I wanted to say I'm sorry."

"I can't talk about this right now."

He glances down at my trembling fingers. "Is there something I can help you with?"

"We aren't friends anymore, remember?"

"Ellie, could we please talk?"

I pinch my lips together and run my hand over my forehead. "I don't think so." I can't get Henry out of my head. His eyes. Those guilt-ridden eyes.

He tucks a wisp of hair behind my ear. I shiver, and his musky scent makes my head spin.

"I'm sorry," he whispers. "I've called a dozen times. I called the day we had the fight."

I don't know what to do. My protective wall begins to crack. My throat closes up, tears pool into my eyes. I shiver and rub my hands over my arms, hugging myself. "I can't deal with this right now."

"I don't want to lose you, Ellie."

A few tears escape. Will gently wipes them from my cheek and cups my chin in his hand. He moves closer. Kissing him could make this all go away. I could pretend I never heard what Henry told me. I could pretend Will and I didn't fight. We could go back to before.

No. There's no going back.

I push his hand away and take a step back. "You can't just show up and pretend everything's OK." I squeeze my eyes shut. "It's not."

Will reaches over and sets a hand on my arm. "I'm not asking you to forget, I'm asking you to accept my apology. That's what friends do, right?"

A warm breeze blows past me. He's right. But I have no idea if he's being honest.

I need to get out of there.

I run off, leaving Will standing there in the doorway of the lighthouse.

the real Henry

I haven't walked into a hospital since the day the ambulance took my mom to the ER, hoping they could still save her life. It's been four months. The memory is so fresh it stings. My heart hurts, aches. Too much nervous energy is pent up inside, I can't swallow.

I want to see if Henry is here. I need to understand what I'm seeing at the lighthouse. I still have the letter from my father in my pocket. It crinkles as I walk.

I count each step up to the main entrance of the hospital. When I get to the top, I stare at my reflection in the glass doors. My hair's hanging over my shoulders, no longer tight in its braid, and my dark almond-shaped eyes have this frightened look.

What am I going to say to the man who stole my life?

At the front desk a pudgy-faced woman with a large backside and a stethoscope around her neck turns to me. "Hi there, honey. What can I do for you?"

"Yes, I um... I was wondering if there's a Henry here?

He's in a coma. I'm hoping to see him."

The nurse scrunches up her face and squints. She sits down at the computer and types for a minute. "Henry Soren?" She types some more. "Is he the nice looking man who fell off that cliff a few months back?"

"I don't know if I'd consider him good-looking, but he did fall off a cliff." I wait for another second. "May I see him?"

She peers at me from behind her computer. "I don't see why not. But you seem a bit young to visit someone with such serious injuries. It might disturb you."

My mom's face flashes before me. *God, this is hard.*

"I'll be OK." I don't mention the fact that I've been seeing Henry's ghost or soul, or whatever it is, wandering around the lighthouse looking for my dead mother. That might disturb *her*.

"It's room number 125. Don't stay more than a few minutes." She stands and points to a hallway. "It's the third door on the right."

I ball up my fists to stop them from shaking. The smell. That plastic, disinfected walls and floors smell. It smells like death to me.

"Listen, you can't stay long," she says. "Ever since this morning, he's been more agitated than normal. I don't want him to get more worked up."

I open my eyes wider. Everything in me stops for a second. How is that possible? The whole thing is getting creepier by the minute. "I'll only stay a short while. I promise."

She opens the door, and I step inside. She leaves me alone in his room. It's bare. No flowers or cards or pictures. I finally get up the courage to glance at him.

I put my hand over my mouth. *No. Way.* The Henry who comes to the lighthouse seems fifty years older than the one lying in the hospital bed. It's the same man, but not him. I take a deep breath and step toward him. This Henry is way younger and much better looking. He doesn't have the wrinkles or crinkly skin. I don't get it.

I take a couple steps toward him, but I don't feel myself moving. "Hi, Henry." I try to sound serious. My voice echoes through the room. "We've met at the lighthouse a few times. I'm Eleanor Martinson. Rose's daughter. I don't think I've told you I'm Rose's daughter." I inch closer. "I know the truth about what you told my mom."

Did his hand just twitch?

I step closer. "Can you hear me?"

I continue talking. I have things I need to say. To the real Henry lying in the bed. "I know you loved her and were jealous of the man from Chile and that you lied. I also know you want to talk to Rose."

I bite my bottom lip and stare at him for a second. With all the tubes, and his battered body, my anger ebbs out. But then my anger rushes back in. My mom's dead. Henry played her like an instrument.

I find my voice. It's raspy, frustrated, unsure of itself. "I even have the letter that Alejandro asked you to give her. I can't believe what you did, Henry. I'm angry. And yet, look at you. You're a wreck. I don't want to feel sorry for you. I want to hate you for ruining my life."

I sit in the chair beside the bed. He's beyond repair. "You lied to get rid of the one man my mom ever loved. It broke my mom. It destroyed her life. Nothing can make that right."

I can't scream at him here, so I bite my bottom lip trying to figure out what to do. The difference between who he is here and who he is at the lighthouse is confusing. I study his features. His light skin. His soft lips. He seems worn down and ravaged at the lighthouse. Here he's handsome and young, despite how wrecked his body is. "Why do you look much older at the lighthouse?"

Maybe it's his soul that's all broken and old? Does a soul look the same as a person's body? Maybe not. Our souls are the most true reflection of who we really are. And, because Henry's in a coma, perhaps his spirit is free to wander around, trying to absolve him.

Is my soul old and decrepit because of my guilt? Is Will's scrunched up and withering because of his anger? I think of Violet, how clear and full of life she is. I can only imagine her soul is the identical twin to her outside self – one and the same.

I can't believe I'm even thinking about these things.

I want to be like Violet. Maybe not the mushy side, but the clear-eyed, no-shame side.

My anger, my rage stand in the way. I can't be like Violet. I have too much guilt.

I clench my fists, but then open them. It all seems so unreal, like I'm only dreaming. I reach out and touch Henry's bedcovers. The white bed sheets are stiff and clean against my fingers.

I can't change what Henry did. It's done. Over.

"Henry, I don't know what to do. The whole thing is crazy. How could you have lied? If you loved Rose, you should have let her go with someone else." My voice is cracking. On the other side of all my anger is such deep sadness. I can't go there. I have to shake this off.

I sit up, lift my chin, and swallow all the guilt and sadness, all those wretched feelings.

"I came here because I wanted to see you. I wanted to know if you were real. And you are. You are real. And what you did was real too."

I pull out the letter from my pocket and grip my father's note till my knuckles are white. Everything is a swirling tornado around me.

Slowly, I slip the letter from the envelope and see my father's handwriting for the first time. It's clean, cursive. Not chicken scratch at all. He wrote only a few lines. I read them aloud, my voice quavering.

Dear Rose,

If you change your mind, you know where to find me. I am going back to Chile. I hope you will decide to call me. I am still in love with you.

If you need to reach me, my address is: Francia 20, Temuco, Chile. And my phone number is 56-21-05-41.

Con amor,

Alejandro Enrique Ramirez

I stare at the words. He sounds nice. I bite my lip to force myself to think of something else.

There's nothing left to say. Or at least, whatever else needs to be said, I'd better say to the other Henry. The tortured one.

"I'll see you later, Henry. Probably at the lighthouse." My voice cracks, but I do my best to hold myself together as I walk out the door.

a step with Maggie

I should feed Maggie. That's a solid thought. I need to center myself, or I'm going to go crazy.

The sunlight fighting its way through the clouds makes the woods sparkle, and the bubbling white clouds cover different patches in the sky, dappling it like a quilt.

In the distance, I can barely make out Henry's shadow. He's about a hundred feet away from me. Our eyes catch for a fleeting moment. A sunray shoots down and hits him straight on. He doesn't disappear. I can still see him, but his body is as thin as papier-mâché.

He nods curtly, and I nod back. Then, he's gone. Shivers run through my whole body. I'm spooked.

A gentle wind blows through the trees, and the clouds thicken. I pick up my speed. *I have to get out of here.* Once I see the lighthouse, I'm more settled. Out of the silence, a loud bark snaps me out of myself. I race down to Maggie's cave.

She's outside pacing back and forth, her eyes big and crazed.

"Maggie," I call out. "It's me, Ellie."

She stops and stares at me.

"It's OK. You're fine, girl."

She calms down, but barely. She growls at me, and the puppies are whining in the back of the cave.

"Take it easy, girl." I take a few steps toward the cave and, for once, she stays still without barking or growling. She's alert, but not aggressive. Hope washes over me.

She and I are within inches of each other. I hold out my hand, staying as still as a rock. She stretches out her nose, barely grazing the top of my hand, and sniffs me. Then she darts back into the cave.

No way. She let me touch her. I knew she'd come around.

I trudge back up the hill and hang out around the lighthouse for a while, gathering energy, thinking, wondering, worrying. Nothing is the way it's supposed to be. Not one thing. Well, except Maggie. I walk back to the farmhouse, still worried.

Alex is standing on the front porch, watching the driveway. As soon as he sees me, he waves with both arms outstretched. Even though I'm tired and want to be alone, I'm actually happy to see Alex and his bright red hair. The tension inside me fades, and I wave back

Alex runs down the porch steps. "Ellie, I've been waiting for you all afternoon. Did your uncle tell you I've been calling?"

"Hey, Alex." I give him a quick wave. "Sorry I haven't called you back. I've been busy."

"I was wondering if you want to hang out tonight?"

I stare at him for a second, trying to think what I should do. After everything I've heard from Aunt Violet, seeing Henry in the woods, visiting the Henry in a coma, and my unresolved conversation with Will – I'm exhausted, but I don't want to be alone yet. I'm afraid to face it all.

Seeing Alex's freckles dance around and his green eyes eager makes me think he might cheer me up. "What'd you have in mind?" I ask.

"I don't know. We could watch a movie or go swimming if you want. Or we could take a walk up to the stargazing hill... whatever."

I glance up at the sky. The temperature has dropped, and the weather is changing. Not to mention my emotional barometer is out of whack. I don't even know how to read my emotions anymore. I pull my phone out to check the time. And to see if anyone's texted. I have at least five texts from Will wanting me to call him. I can't talk to him right now. "How about a movie?"

"Do you want to come over for dinner?" His smile is so wide I can count his teeth.

"I better eat with the family, but I'll walk over after I help with the dishes."

He agrees and then runs across the pasture. I go around to the kitchen door.

Violet is washing lettuce in the sink. She gives me a kind nod. One that says she cares. "How are you doing Ellie?"

I shut the door. "I hardly know anymore."

"I'm sorry you have to deal with all this," she says. "It's not right."

"Didn't anyone ever tell you? Life isn't fair." I give her a forced smile. I don't want to talk about it. "Do you need me to do anything?"

She shakes her head a couple times but then stops herself. "Can you set the table?"

I think Violet knows nothing is going to make this easier.

I take the silverware out of the drawer. I can't decide whether I want to tell her about Alejandro's letter. But how do I tell her I found the letter without telling her about Henry?

I have no reason to mistrust Aunt Violet, but I don't think I should tell her I've been seeing Henry's spirit wandering around the lighthouse. She might try to keep me from going back. It also might make her worry about my sanity. Which is understandable. I'm starting to worry about my sanity too.

the night before the party

Walking over to Alex's house, I wish I hadn't been so impulsive. When I said I'd hang out with Alex, it sounded like a good idea to keep my mind off Will, my mom, Henry... but now I'm regretting it.

Alex's mom answers the door when I knock. Her hair is slightly darker than Alex's. "Ellie, glad you could make it. Come on in." She waves for me to step inside.

She's holding her phone and has juice stains on her shirt. She starts walking toward the kitchen but turns back to say, "Alex will be down in a minute."

She disappears, and I stand in the hallway until Alex comes out holding five different movies.

"Hey, Ellie," he says. "Do you want popcorn and ice cream, or just popcorn?"

"Both, definitely."

"Chick flick or action?"

"Action, please." I can't handle anything sappy that will make me cry.

Upstairs in the media room, they have a flat screen

TV and a surround-sound system that's even better than a movie theatre.

We decide on the *The Two Towers*, and I immediately think of Will and how he was reading those books at the beginning of the summer. He wanted to talk to me earlier. *Should I call him?* No.

Alex stands up. "I'll pop the popcorn before we start the movie. Be right back."

"Should I go with you?" I don't want to sit alone upstairs. It'll only make me think of Will.

"Sure."

Downstairs, during all the popping and pinging in the microwave, Alex turns and stares at me as if he's trying to muster up his courage.

I get the impression he didn't just want to hang out tonight.

His expression is serious, and he rubs his arm like he's nervous. "Ellie, before we go back upstairs, could we talk?"

Oh, boy. This can't be good.

He stands there with such honest eyes, and his freckles, which are so big and bold, make him seem innocent.

"Sure. What's up?" I cross my arms over my chest and rest against the counter, forcing myself not to bolt out the door. I can't handle any more emotional drama.

"Oh, never mind." He reaches for the popcorn and pours it all into a bowl so quickly, kernels tumble over the side. We both pick the pieces off the floor.

Alex pulls some paper towels off the rack. "Let's go upstairs and watch the movie."

I breathe a sigh of relief.

The media room faces east, so it's one of the first rooms to get dark in the evening. I sit on the corner of the couch and pull my feet underneath me. Alex sits as close as possible without being too obvious. He keeps creeping toward me and fixing his shorts, like they're hiking up.

Finally, we're inches apart, sharing a bowl of popcorn,

and our hands keep grazing. My stomach twists, and my hands get sweaty. I don't want to hurt him, or our friendship, especially after the way Will has hurt me, but I'm not interested in Alex in that way.

Before I know it, in between picking up buttered popcorn, his fingers lace through mine. *Gulp.* We sit there for a moment, and I almost let it go. After all, holding hands isn't kissing or anything. But I don't want to get mixed up in a big mess.

I excuse myself to go to the bathroom across the hall. I wash my hands and dry them and stare at myself in the mirror for a minute to convince myself that letting him down easily won't be the end of the world. We'll be fine.

When I come back to the couch, I sit farther away from him. Within minutes, he's closer. He arches back and rests his arm on the back of the couch. Then ever so slowly, he lowers his arm onto my shoulders.

My stomach tosses and turns. I stare hard at the movie. I swallow about five hundred times, licking my lips. Then, I realize he might misinterpret the lip-licking, and I stop. All I want to do is go back to the farmhouse. I should never have said we could hang out. I'm exhausted, tired, and not ready to deal with this.

Right when I'm about ready to get up and call it a night, Alex scoots over, cups my face in his hands, and kisses me before I can react.

Then he touches my cheek. "I've wanted to do that all summer," he whispers in this really sweet voice that takes me by surprise.

He smells good. His lips felt nice. And he tasted like the perfect combination of mint gum and buttery popcorn.

"Alex, I wasn't expecting that." I touch my lips, but I'm so taken aback I can't move my legs or my arms. I stare at the couch and clear my throat.

On the movie, Aragorn is yelling at the Orcs.

I have to get out of here. Now.

Alex squeezes my hand. "I haven't told you how I

feel about you because I thought you liked Will, but Amy said you two weren't talking anymore. I decided to take my chances. I really like you, Ellie." He moves to kiss me again without even waiting for my response.

I hold my hands in front of my chest and stiffen. "Hold on, Alex. I need to think about this." I pause and force myself to look into his eyes. "I'm sorry. I care about you, but I'd like to be friends." I said the exact same thing to Will only a few days ago. But with Alex, it's the whole truth.

"This would be like the best way to improve our friendship." He raises his eyebrows.

I wiggle my hand out of his grip. "I should go home. I'll see you at the party tomorrow?"

"Let me walk you home, Ellie."

"That's OK. It only takes a minute. I'll be fine." *I hope.*

I run down the stairs without glancing back. I open his front door, hurry down the steps, and race to the farmhouse.

This is getting way too complicated.

In the kitchen, Ben is sitting at the table drinking a tall glass of milk and has three cookies on a plate. Who knows how many he's already eaten.

"You look flushed," he says. "Want some cookies?"

"Hey, Ben." I take a deep breath, trying to regain my composure. "Cookies and milk sound great."

He stands and, with a flourish, removes a handful of cookies from the cookie jar, pours milk into a giant mug, and sets it all down in front of me. The fresh sugar cookies Violet made earlier. So light and fluffy, I could eat a dozen.

We eat in silence, and he hardly even glances at me, but I can tell he's aware that I'm flustered and is trying to make me feel comfortable. That's how Ben is. Sitting here at the table with his gentle kindness and willingness to let me sit in silence makes me understand how Violet fell in love with him. He's the nicest man I've ever met.

After I eat two cookies and drink half of my milk, Ben

speaks up. He keeps his eyes on his glass. "I'm guessing Alex told you how he feels about you?"

"Yes." I take a long sip of milk. "How did you know?"

Ben bites into another cookie and waits until he swallows to speak. "He's asked about you every day for the last week. I figured he was working up the courage."

"I don't want to hurt his feelings. He's a nice guy."

Ben reaches over and sets his big hand on my shoulder. "You need to do whatever you think is right, but what about Will?"

"What happened with Will is over."

"Really?"

I take a sip of my milk. "Yes. Why wouldn't it be?"

"Because he's called you more times than I can count. You raise your eyebrows and almost freeze every time you hear his name. Seems like whatever started with Will won't be over for quite some time."

I scowl at my plate. "I don't understand boys like Will," I finally say. "He pushed me all summer to be his friend, and then when I do something he doesn't like, he pushes me away."

"Boys like Will are scared of girls like you." Ben stands and sets his plate in the sink.

"Why in the world would Will be scared of me?" I return the milk to the refrigerator.

He reaches over and sets his hand on my head in a tender way.

My eyes get misty.

"That's something you'll have to ask Will."

"I guess." I give him a slight grin. "Thanks for the milk and cookies." I duck my head. I don't want him see I'm fighting tears.

"You're welcome. Cookies always make me feel better."

We tiptoe up the stairs to keep from waking anyone. Ben goes into his bedroom, and I climb the stairs to my room. I'm not sure how to deal with Will. I miss him. A lot.

But I refuse to be one of those girls who gives in because she needs to have a guy. I won't do it. But he's been my friend. And I've been telling him to forgive his dad. Maybe I should practice what I preach.

I toss and turn until I finally fall asleep. I dream of Orcs and Will and Alex. Strange dreams.

summer party

The next morning when I wake up, it's suffocatingly warm in the attic. I'm exhausted, and a ball of desperation sits in the pit of my stomach. I need to talk to someone about Henry and Alejandro.

I forgot about Alex for a few minutes, but as I emerge from my groggy state, I remember he kissed me and that Ben said it's not over with Will.

I prop myself up, put my hands behind my head, and stare at the ceiling. The sun's morning rays are shooting into my bedroom through the far window. Violet is rustling about with the kids, and Ben's stomping through the house. He moves in large, slow motions, and each one seems to leave its mark wherever he lands.

I pitter-patter downstairs to the middle floor, which is also warmer than usual. The humidity in the air mixed with the heat is almost intolerable. My hair becomes even more curly and frizzy than normal before it rains. This morning it looks like an eagle's nest. I grab the frizz and shove it into a tight knot. The tiny wisps around my face make tight curls all around my face.

Violet and Ben are discussing something. "I need to go today, Ben," Violet says. "I told you this a few weeks ago. And I don't like asking Ellie to watch the kids all day. It's not fair to her. You told me you'd take the day off work." Her voice aches with frustration.

"Vi, there's nothing I can do about it. I was hoping to take the day off, but I have to work. I'm sorry. Ellie will have to watch the kids. She won't mind."

I don't mind at all. It'll give me something to do with my day, besides worry about Will and Alex. I didn't have any plans except to check on Maggie, but I can go later. I rush downstairs and into the early morning chaos of breakfast. The kids are eating cereal, dishes are everywhere, crayons are strewn about, a box of apples sits on the floor ready to be made into applesauce.

"I'd be happy to watch the kids, Violet."

Violet has her arms crossed. A slight frown creases her forehead. "Ellie, you had a hard day yesterday. Are you sure you can handle the kids?"

"I'm sure. Yesterday was hard. But I've had worse days."

Ben looks at me, "Thanks, Ellie. I'll be back in time for you to go to the party."

I smile at my aunt and uncle. "No problem." As Violet grins back at me, the phone rings.

I pick up. "Hello. Parker house."

"Ellie?" comes Amy's voice.

"Hey, Amy. Don't worry. I'm planning on going to the party."

Her voice has this electric energy. "Nadine's spending the night at my house, and I thought it'd be fun if you'd come too. The guys are all going camping."

Since Will isn't going to be there, it might actually be fun to hang out with just the girls. Before I can answer, she adds softly, "Who knows, maybe we could even sneak out or something."

I cringe. "Let me ask." I cover the phone carefully so Amy can't hear the answer. "Amy's having a slumber party. Is it OK if I go?"

Uncle Ben turns around and squints. "What about Will? Are you comfortable with that?"

Ben's such a nice guy, always taking care of everyone. I whisper, "He's going camping."

Ben nods. "It's up to you, Ellie." He keeps working on the kids to finish their breakfast.

I put the phone back up to my ear. "I can come."

"Oh, good. Why don't you come early, and I'll straighten your hair?"

I hate straightening my hair. It's such a waste of time. "I'll come early, but I'm not sure I want to straighten my hair."

"I'll do it for you. This is an important party. Everyone will be there. Come around five."

"I'm watching the kids today, so I may not make it. If not, I'll just meet you at the party, OK?"

"Really try, Ellie. I want to do your hair and makeup."

I start worrying. I don't wear makeup. Ever. "We'll see. I'll be at your house as soon as I can. Bye, Amy."

"Oh and Ellie, charge your phone – so people can actually get ahold of you."

"Sure." I hang up.

Aunt Violet is staring at me, laughing. "She's making you exhausted before you even get to her house. Her mom used to be the exact same way with me."

"Are you kidding? Julie used to be like Amy?"

My aunt nods. "She was the beauty queen, the prom queen, the cheerleader, and the girl everyone wanted to be with. She and your mom used to fight over attention."

"I'm not seeing that at all. She doesn't seem the beauty-queen type."

"Life shaped her differently than she would have liked, but she's still a treasure."

"Yeah, but I don't see her acting like Amy. Amy thinks she and her mom have nothing in common."

Aunt Violet grabs her purse and opens the back door. "Amy doesn't want to accept that her parents' divorce broke her heart just as much as it broke her mother's and her brother's. She's trying to hide behind a veneer of beauty and sweetness. It won't hold."

Once again, I can't believe how quick she is. Nothing gets past her.

Violet steps out of the house. "See you tomorrow. Have a good time at the party, and thanks for taking care of the kids." She turns to the kids. "Be good. I'll be on the seven o'clock ferry."

I ruffle Gabe's hair. "We're going to have a great day, aren't we?"

Violet runs out to the car, waving good-bye in her frantic sort of way. When Ben comes down, he grabs his truck keys from the table. "Ellie, don't feel bad if you have to call me. I'll try to be home as soon as I get done. I'm hoping around four this afternoon. We'll see."

"It's no problem if I don't go to Amy's early. She just wants to do my hair and stuff. Whatever time you get here is fine."

He gives me a side hug. "Thanks. Call me if you need anything."

I nod and grin. The kids hug him, and he leaves.

"What do you want to do all day?" I ask, putting my hands on my hips after he walks out the door.

"Build a fort," Mikey says. "A big one." Gabe and Prissy nod.

"You'll have to help me find all the blankets or sheets in the linen closet and start pushing the chairs from the kitchen into the living room."

The kids cheer and run around to get everything. Hanging out with the kids is the perfect distraction.

In the afternoon after they've gone down for their naps, I go upstairs to pack.

It's starting to mist.

Ben is late, but not too late. He comes running into the house, shaking his jacket, and glancing out the window. The wind is blowing.

"Ellie?" he calls out. "Do you want me to take you to Amy's?"

"Sure. Thanks." I grab Prissy, and Ben whisks the boys into his arms.

They all smush together into the middle of the seat.

"How was your day?" he asks the kids.

Gabe claps. "We made a fort, Daddy!"

"We laughed a lot," Prissy tells him.

Ben glances over at me. "When you got here, I never pictured you'd spend the day laughing. A few months ago, I wasn't sure if you'd ever smile again. You've changed."

I have changed. Slowly, the way the sun comes up in the morning, it's up and out before you know it. I don't feel like the same person who arrived on the island a few months ago. "They bring out the best in me."

He turns onto Main Street and stops in front of Amy's store. "Honey," he says, "you bring out the best in everyone. Have a good time tonight. Call me if you need anything. Even if you need me to get you really late. No questions asked."

I know he means it. "Thanks, Ben. I'll see you tomorrow around lunchtime."

Off in the distance, a low rumble of thunder rolls off the hills. The sky fills with black clouds. I jump out of the truck, waving at the kids.

The doorbell chimes when I open the café door. For some reason I figured it would be Julie, but Will's standing behind the counter engrossed in a book. When he realizes it's me, he lowers the book and gives me the mischievous smile that always sends tingles down my spine. It's the look that makes me think he knows all my secrets or makes me want to confide all my secrets. I press my lips together to prevent a smile, but I think my eyes give it away. I have a lot I want to talk about. He doesn't know anything about Alejandro's letter, or about Henry, or anything. I wish we could go on a long walk to the lighthouse. Then I could spill everything.

But I remember we aren't talking and that he threw me out of his room and acted like a total jerk. I try to hide how much I want to talk to him and attempt to only act sort-of interested. "Hey, Will." I give him a half wave.

"Hey, you," he says. "How is everything?"

"It's OK" I glance at his book. "What're you reading?"

"*Jane Eyre.*"

"Why?"

"Someone told me it was her favorite book. I wanted to see why."

I gulp. "Did you figure it out?"

He nods. "I think so."

I seriously think I'm in love with this guy. I try to concentrate. Who reads *Jane Eyre* because of a girl? "What part are you on?"

He picks up the old battered copy. "The part when Jane finds Mr. Rochester at the end."

We look at each other for a moment.

Before I can add anything, he says, "It was hard for Jane. But in the end she was happy, wasn't she?"

"I think she was. I better go and see Amy. She wants to straighten my hair." His face crinkles up as if I said I was going to shave my head or something.

I shrug and go toward the side stairs leading up to his mom's apartment. "Something she wants to try is all."

"Oh. Can we talk at the party?" he asks. "I'm leaving in a few minutes to help the guys set up the food and the tent and everything."

"Yeah, we can talk." I'm already halfway up the stairs. I peer over the railing.

"I need to tell you something," he says.

"OK." I wonder what he wants to tell me. I wish I could tell him about Alejandro and Henry, but I'm not sure I should.

I knock on the door, and Amy opens it in a rush. She yanks me toward her room. I hardly even have a chance to say *hi* to her mom as we pass. Julie is sitting at the kitchen table going over a bunch of papers.

Once Amy slams the bedroom door, she says with a tell-me-everything tone, "What in the world is going on with you and Alex? I mean just the other day it's my brother, and then you two have a fight or something, and now you're hooking up with Alex? For someone shy and quiet, you certainly have a way of getting around."

I am appalled. "What are you talking about?"

She shakes a finger at me. "Don't play innocent with me, girl. Alex told Jake, who of course told me, how you two kissed last night!" She tucks her hair behind her ear, her expression intense. I feel like my back is pinned to a wall.

"I didn't want anyone to know about the Alex thing."

"Ellie, Alex has had a crush on you all summer. If you thought he was going to keep your kiss a secret, you were wrong. Most girls think boys don't kiss and tell, but they do."

She sits on the bed. "What is it with you two? And I must say I'm glad you're done with my brother. I didn't want you two together in the first place. You two couldn't be more different. Besides, he and Nadine are back together. And you've got Alex." She makes a wide sweeping motion with her hand.

It's like a gust of icy wind blew into my face. I can't breathe. "He and Nadine are back together?"

"Nadine told me. They talked it all through this morning. I'm glad. You two weren't right together."

I take a deep breath. I have to focus hard. My stomach is churning, my throat tightens, and this pain squeezes my heart. It's different from the pain with my mom, but also constricting.

"What exactly did Nadine tell you?"

"She said it's pretty much a done deal. They're going to the party together and everything. And you'll be with Alex."

My throat's closing, and I can't talk. I need to get out of her house and go home. What was I thinking agreeing to hang out with her and have a slumber party with Nadine? I want to hide out in my lighthouse.

I make an effort to hold it together. "Alex and I aren't together. It was one kiss. I don't like Alex that way."

Amy puts her hand on my arm. "I totally think you should give it a chance."

"It's not like that with Alex." My voice comes out like a raspy whisper.

"Have a little fun, Ellie. Lighten up."

I stare at the wood floors. I almost run out of her house to find Alex and scream at him for telling everyone we kissed. And Will did say he had something to tell me. Maybe he wanted to explain about him and Nadine. But that doesn't explain why was he reading *Jane Eyre*. He probably planned to say we should be friends, like I wanted all along. If I'd just listened to my heart at the beginning of the summer, none of this would have happened.

"Are you ready to do your hair?" Amy asks, completely unaware that I'm desperately trying not to cry, that my heart is even more broken than it was before.

I swallow. I breathe in and stuff it all back down. "Yes."

She settles me the chair at her vanity. "It's going to take us forever to straighten all your curls out." She runs her fingers through my hair.

When she finishes, she turns me toward the mirror. "What do you think?"

Clearly, she loves what she's done, and it doesn't matter to her that I'm unrecognizable to myself. She only cares whether I look pretty or not.

I run my hands over my hair. "Wow, who is that person in the mirror?"

"Isn't it cool?" She touches my hair like its foreign silk.

I try not to roll my eyes. "Thanks, Amy." I turn away from the mirror. "Let's get dressed and go." I just want this night to be over.

Amy takes off her T-shirt and slides on a cute jean skirt. "Why you don't just go with the Alex thing?" She pulls a shirt over her head. "If it doesn't work out in a few weeks, break it off. It's not like you're married or anything."

"I don't like him like that. I can't lie to him."

Amy grabs a light jacket and then turns. "Ellie, sometimes you're too old-fashioned. I mean look at me and Jake. We're just fooling around. Nothing serious. At the end of the summer, it's over, and we're none the worse for it."

"I'm not interested in relationships like that." I start for the door. I know she's serious, but I wonder if she really is none the worse for it. Will and I kissed one time, and my stomach has been in knots ever since.

When we walk downstairs, Julie's at the cash register. She grins when she sees us. "Ellie, your hair looks lovely. Amy did a nice job."

I give her a half smile. "Thanks."

Amy jumps in. "Mom, don't forget that Nadine and Ellie are staying the night. We'll be home around midnight."

"Have a good time. Make sure you let me know when you get home."

We wave, and then we're out the door. It's still only drizzling outside, but the wind has picked up. The trees are blowing in large waving motions, and dust is swirling in midair. The breeze smells of fresh wet concrete. Amy forces me to put my hood on. She swears she'll never do my hair again if I let the rain ruin it.

Jake lives close to Main Street. We only have to run for a minute or two. His family lives on the main floor of a huge house, and all the guests take the top and bottom.

My stomach pitches up and down as we walk to the back, through the side gate. We follow the trail of white twisted lights, twinkling around the trees like an invitation.

When I get there, I'm totally surprised. A white tent is sitting in the middle of the backyard. Even though the wind is blowing and it's raining, underneath the canopy, it's dry and warm. Round tables are scattered around, a huge table with punch and finger food makes it look like a wedding reception, the ones I've seen on TV, but have never actually attended. People are mingling around. Some, I'd seen at the lake, and others, I'm guessing, have been away for the summer. No one here grew up in a trailer park, that's for sure. I'm more out of place right now than I've been all summer.

Will is off in the distance talking to Nadine. Her hair is hanging down straight as an arrow, much like mine, except on her, it fits. She's wearing a short skirt, and her tanned legs seem to go on for miles. I stare at them longer than I should. I wonder how Will feels. My stomach twists and turns. Part of me wants to run out of the party and never be seen again, and the other part of me wants to go over and beat the crap out of Nadine.

Standing there next to Amy and staring at Nadine, I wish I hadn't let Amy do my hair, because I don't feel like myself. I feel like a fake. Will and Nadine glance our way, and they both nod. Except Will's eyes don't change when he sees me, there's no delight or mischievous knowing. My stomach drops.

I force myself to turn around. Alex and Jake are standing on chairs, putting up the last few lights. Jake looks good, and Amy sighs when she sees him.

"Isn't he gorgeous, Ellie?"

"He is pretty good-looking." I'm totally distracted. I can hardly focus on Amy's words.

"And he absolutely adores me."

"I thought it wasn't serious?"

"Sure, but I can still think he's hot, can't I?"

"He really likes you, Amy."

"Do you think so?" she asks, and I see what Violet meant. Behind Amy's outer layer of it-doesn't-matter are the same insecurities we all have.

"Yeah, I do."

She sighs again and waves. Jake looks like he's trying hard to finish hanging lights and not race over to her. I hope Amy doesn't end up hurting him. But by the way Amy's gazing at him, with her head all tipped to the side and biting her bottom lip, he's pretty safe from heartbreak, at least for a while.

Jake comes over and hugs Amy. Then their hands interlock.

"Hey, Ellie," Jake says. "Your hair looks nice."

"Thanks," I tell him. "And thanks for inviting me to your party. It's amazing back here."

"Sometimes it's nice that my parents run a bed and breakfast, because they have all the stuff for big events. This party is their end of summer gift to us for putting up with a house full of people we don't know."

"It's a great gift." I glance around the room.

Alex comes from the back of the tent, holding an extension cord.

"Hey, Ellie." He steps past Jake to stand next to me. "Your hair looks nice. You should do it like that more often."

I silently rub my hands over it again. Alex has no idea who I really am.

"Could we talk in private for a few minutes?" I beckon with my head and walk toward the back of the tent.

When we reach a spot where no one can hear us, I turn around and cross my arms. I want to be nice, but I'm annoyed and can't hide it. "Alex, have you been telling people we're getting together?"

He steps back. "Geez, Ellie, you don't have to be so abrupt."

"Sorry, Alex, I didn't mean to be rude. I was just

wondering how Amy found out you kissed me last night?"

He rubs his forehead. "I just told a few people is all. I'm sorry I said anything about us. I mean, before you had the chance."

My face heats, and I unfold my arms and then fold them again. His eyes are kind. My heart softens as I realize how hopeful he is. I need to say this like I care. "Alex, we aren't together. I should have been more direct with you last night, but I didn't want to hurt your feelings. The thing is... I don't want to be anything more than friends."

He gets this very confused look on his face. "But we kissed last night."

"Alex, you kissed me, and then I got up and went home."

"I thought that was because it took you by surprise."

"That's true. I was definitely surprised. I'm sorry, and I should have been more honest. You are a good friend."

He hangs his head. "You still like Will, don't you?"

I frown. "I don't know, but I'm not doing this because of him."

"That's good, because Jake told me that Will and Nadine are hooking back up."

My world goes dark for a second. I gulp and shift my stance. "Will and I are just friends," I squeak out.

"I hope that's true. I don't want you to get hurt."

"I can take care of myself," I say, trying to catch my breath. "Are we still friends?"

"Of course." He hugs me in a totally platonic way. "I should have waited to see what you were feeling. Besides, if you stay here for the school year, I'll have plenty of time to convince you otherwise."

"Alex." I hit him gently on the shoulder. I can tell we're still friends. "You ready to go back to the party?"

"Yeah. Guess I've got to find another girl to flirt with."

I can't tell which part is serious and which part is a joke. But it's fine. At least everything's OK between us.

When we turn around and weave back through the

crowd, couples are slow dancing. Jake is running his fingers through Amy's hair and whispering something in her ear while they dance. Her eyes are closed, and she's resting her head on his shoulder.

In the distance, Will and Nadine are slow dancing. Her face is nestled into his neck, and she seems as happy as I've ever seen her. Will's eyes are focused on the floor, but as I stare at him, he glances up, and our eyes meet. He stares at me without any emotion, not even a shrug. I stand there like a fool for way too long. Hot tears burn my cheeks. When did I start crying? I turn away so no one can see.

It's hopeless. We'll never be close again.

I'm supposed to go to a slumber party with Nadine tonight. Amy is totally going to ask her a bunch of questions. This is the whole reason I didn't want to get involved with Will in the first place. I didn't want to get hurt. I wipe my eyes. The salt of my tears leaves a bitter taste on my lips.

If we'd stayed friends, the whole Nadine thing wouldn't matter. But we kissed, and he cried in my arms. We can't change that. We can't change anything. I race out of the tent, away from the party, and run and run and run.

The wind and rain blast through my troubled heart. The rain pelts down, mingling with my tears. Then my mom's face flashes before my eyes. I see her in our trailer. I see the hopelessness in her eyes and how she shook when I yelled at her. Henry flashes into my mind. And the man from Chile. My father. It's all too much. I can't handle it anymore.

I run hard and fast, trying to escape all the pain. But I realize it's never going to go away. I've been running away since my mom died: running from my guilt, my anger, from my sadness. But it's all still there.

I have to face this. I have to face the truth of what I

yelled at her that horrible day. I said cruel things. It's my
fault. It's time to tell the truth, even if only to the wind.

the great storm

My internal storm comes to a raging head on the same night as one of the biggest storms I've ever seen – as if I needed a physical crisis to bring my internal chaos into clarity.

The rain and winds are ferocious. The tree branches whip around like leather ropes. Leaves tear off and whirl into the dark sky. Black clouds ring out water like someone squeezing a sponge.

Oh no. Maggie. Her small cave won't survive such a big storm. Water is probably pooling in her cave already. I have to get to her and the pups before they drown.

I race toward the cave.

My hair curls into a tangled, spiraled mess. My eyes burn. My arms flail as I trip over debris, duck under tree branches, dodge swirling leaves. I can barely see through the rain. I finally get to the path that leads to the lighthouse. If I hadn't walked this path so many times, I never would have found my way in the driving rain.

I rush past the lighthouse to the beach trail. It's

washing away. I grab onto bushes and small trees, slipping and sliding downhill. Water streams down the cliff, and the sea crashes in large foaming waves against the rocks. Salt spray stings my eyes, blurring my vision. I struggle down thirty feet, drenched and covered in mud. The tide has risen so high, water is already beating against the cliff wall and splashing into Maggie's cave. She and the pups will be trapped.

I crawl as close as I dare. "Maggie," I scream. My voice disappears into the wind.

Within seconds, Maggie darts to the cave entrance, her hackles raised. She snarls and paces. Her eyes are wild with frenzy. That dog is not going to come near me.

In the back of the cave, the pups shriek and yelp. If I don't do something fast, they're going to die. They don't have the strength to swim through the current. I've worked for two months to convince that dog I'm a friend, but she's acting like I'm some stranger she's never seen before.

I grip a sapling next to the cave and reach for the scruff of her neck. Maggie bares her teeth and jerks her head around to bite me.

I won't leave them to die. I can't leave them.

I grab for Maggie's neck again. She whips her head around, saliva dripping from her mouth, and attacks. I yank my hand away and lose my balance, tumbling backward. My arms pinwheel in the air before I can grip a tree to catch my balance.

Behind me, someone calls, "Eleanor!"

I turn. Will's there, right behind me. His hair is plastered to his forehead, and his soggy shirt is clinging to his chest. "I knew you'd try to save the dog." He glances at Maggie. "Let me help you."

I don't want to deal with Will right now. I shake my head and wave him away. "I don't want your help."

Will steps closer. "Try to grab her again," he says. "The pups will die if we don't get her. They won't survive this storm. This cave's almost under water."

I wipe the tears from my eyes, but everything's still blurry. "Why won't she come? I've tried so hard all summer. She should trust me."

"She's too wounded. Her hurt has nothing to do with you."

The wind whirls, cracking a tree branch overhead. It crashes to the ground and rolls off the cliff. The waves splash higher.

I let go of the tree trunk, gain my balance, and then, taking two quick steps toward Maggie, I plan to scoop her up from behind, so she can't bite me. If I can get her into my arms, maybe she'll calm down. *Please, let me help you, Maggie.*

I reach for Maggie's neck with one hand and try to sweep up her back legs with the other. She thrusts her neck out and snarls. I jump back, but Maggie lunges. I swerve out of her path.

She tumbles off the cliff into the storm's darkness.

"No," I scream. My voice terrifies me. It's filled with a I wake to desperation I've never heard before. Absolute despair. I fall to my knees and rip up clods of wet grass next to me. "I have to go find her. Maybe she's still alive."

"Ellie, we need to get the pups. You did everything you could. She's gone."

I shake my head in quick, manic movements. "How do you know? She might be wounded, and we could save her."

"The beach is torn up down there." His voice is strong, loud, and sure. "Maggie is gone. But we can still get the pups."

"I can't leave her." My voice cracks. "I have to help her." I crawl toward the edge.

Will grabs my arm. "Get the puppies, Ellie."

A gust of wind rips past and almost blows me off the hill.

Will steadies me. "I'll go down and look for Maggie."

I grip the tree trunk for a second as Will disappears

into the darkness below.

Then, I crawl on the wet ground toward the cave and fumble my way inside. Water's sloshing across the cave floor.

Strands of soaked hair are suction-cupped to my cheeks.

The pups are whimpering in the back, snuggled close together. I reach for one; its black coat is wet and chilly. I tuck it under my arm. The other two are brown and white. They're shivering. Their tiny little bodies calm in my arms. They still tremble, but less than before.

I inch backward out of the cave, hoping Will can find their mother, that she's still alive somehow.

When I can stand, I shuffle out of the cave, trying to hold it together, but my despair and grief are raging underneath, begging for release.

Will stumbles up the hill. He's holding Maggie's limp body in his arms.

"We'll put her somewhere safe and bury her tomorrow," he says.

When his eyes meet mine, it's the human contact, the way Will conveys his compassion, that tips me over the edge, and the tears unlock again. In the frenzy of saving Maggie, I had to focus on her, try to save her, but now, with her gone, sorrow surges inside, despondency washes over me. Darkness. A whole lot of darkness. A loud, awful cry escapes.

We struggle up the hill, water streaming down it. I can't see in front of me. The puppies squirm, and I scramble to keep my balance. I squeeze them tighter than I should, because I'm so afraid I'll drop them. They whimper and squirm. We stumble forward, the rain pelting down. The wind is howling. I slip on the mud.

"Will," I scream.

In a flash, he grabs my arm and steadies me, cradling Maggie in his other arm. Her body brushes against me. I lurch forward and cry out.

"Are you OK?" Will's voice is fierce.

"I don't know." My voice sounds shattered. Tears intermingle with the rain down my cheeks. The wind is roaring, but nothing compares to the anguish roaring inside me. I can't pull myself together. I'm holding the puppies, but I'm frozen. Maggie is dead. Will is holding her dead body. Nothing I did all summer mattered. She died anyway. Why does it always come to death?

"Ellie, we need to get the puppies warm. Take them to the lighthouse." His commanding voice forces me to pay attention.

I do what he says, but hopelessness grips me.

I carry the pups to the cottage, hunched against the howling wind. Tears scald my eyes. Will lays Maggie outside the door. "Don't look at her. Just get the pups into the house. They need you."

Once inside the cottage, I set the pups in the corner and find some towels. I try to wipe the excess water off them. My hands are shaking so much I can hardly grip the towel. I'm shivering, shuddering. I squeeze my hands together to control them. But they won't stop. My body is coming undone.

Will comes up behind me and drapes a blanket around my shoulder. I wrap it around myself, staring at the three motherless puppies whining and squirming.

I scoop the black one into my arms. She's a little girl. "I know, little one. My mom's dead too. That was my fault too." I stroke her damp fur with shaky hands. I'm trembling, and I can't stop. "I'll take care of you."

Will goes to the cupboard and brings out the dog food.

He puts out bowls of food and water. Then he gently lifts the black puppy from my arms and sets her down with the other pups in the blanket, and they go to sleep wrapped together.

Will helps me to my feet and guides me over to sit against the wall.

I sink to the floor. My clothes drip, forming puddles

around me, and I still can't stop shivering. I'm damp and cold, but the trembling is from the earthquake inside me. The tears start again.

Will sits next to me. He's close, but keeping his distance. He lets me cry for a while before saying anything. "I'm sorry she fell, Eleanor."

"It's my fault," I tell him. "I swerved. I shouldn't have swerved."

"No, you had no choice. Besides, her problems came from something before she ever knew you."

"I tried so hard to help her, but it didn't work. It made no difference."

"Ellie, those puppies are alive because of you."

I shake my head. "No. Don't you see? It never makes any difference. She's dead. Maggie's dead. My mom is dead."

"I know. I'm so sorry."

Will's voice is kind, but I'm not even paying attention to him. "I tried. My whole life. So hard." I'm wailing, getting louder with every word. "Every day when I came home from school, I'd hide her bottles, stash her needles. I'd stash everything, dump the vodka down the toilet. I begged her to give it up. I was afraid every day of my life."

Will moves closer. He puts his hand on my arm and nods as if he understands. "Ellie, that wasn't your fault."

I shake my head and brush tears from my eyes. I can't hold the tears back anymore. "You don't know that." My voice is edging on panic. "I haven't told you everything. I haven't told you the truth. I haven't told anyone."

Will shakes his head. "No matter what you tell me, it wasn't your fault, Eleanor."

His assurance makes me angry. He doesn't know anything. He doesn't know the truth.

"I told her I hated her."

"We say lots of things when we're angry."

My voice echoes through the lighthouse. I'm shouting, yelling at Will, but I don't see him. My eyes are blurry, and

I'm back in my trailer, a scared and frightened little girl. "But it was true. I did hate her. I wanted to be free from all the pain and fear. I wanted it over."

I wipe my eyes and focus on Will.

His eyes are so kind, so filled with pain. "That wasn't your fault. You can't blame yourself for all that."

"Didn't you hear me? I'm a horrible person. Who hates their own mother?"

"Lots of people when they're upset."

His reassurance makes me furious. Why isn't he listening to me?

He grips my shoulders. "I hated my dad for leaving my mom. But I can't change what happened, and neither can you. We have to accept what is... and figure out how to go on with our lives."

"At least your parents are alive. Death is permanent, Will. It's over. Nothing I ever do will change it."

"Ellie, that doesn't mean your life is over."

I hang my head. "Nothing I do makes a difference."

"Yes it does. You saved three puppies. You took an old, worn out lighthouse and made it beautiful again. And you've made friends with people who love you."

"But it wasn't enough." My voice is tired, defeated. I gaze at him. "Why are you here, Will? I thought you and Nadine were back together?"

"Nadine? No. I only danced with her because Alex said you two were getting together."

"That was a big misunderstanding." I sigh and lower my head, grip the blanket tighter around me to try to contain myself. "I want to tell you something else about my mom. I want you to hear it. But I'm still angry at you."

He scoots closer and stares into my eyes. "I'm sorry. For everything. I was scared and upset because you were the first person I respected who had the guts to tell me the truth. Please forgive me, Ellie. Please. I'm ready to hear whatever you need to tell me."

"I found out stuff about my mom, and the disappearing old man, and about my dad."

He sits up straighter. "Tell me."

So I do. I tell him the whole story, the story of how my mother fell in love with Alejandro, about how my dad loved my mom, about how Henry came between them, about how he lied.

Will listens and never interrupts. He stares at me, absolutely still.

I finish and then say, "But there's more, Will. I need to tell you more. About what happened before I moved here."

He reaches out and squeezes my hand.

I hang my head and swallow, then take a deep breath. I have to finish my story. I have to tell him everything. "I was saving up for a car... An Outback, actually."

He blinks and understanding flashes in his eyes.

I tell him about the drug dealer and, before he can try to comfort me, I spit out the rest. "Later that day, after she got back, we had a huge fight. I told her about giving the money to her drug dealer. I screamed at her that I was fed up with taking care of her and making sure she woke up in the morning. Tired of paying her freaking bills. I told her I was sick of it all. And then I screamed that I hated her and wished..." *I can't get the words out.* A few tears roll down my cheeks. I stare at my hands.

Say it, Ellie. You have to say it out loud. "I wished..." I squeeze my eyes shut. *Breathe, Ellie. Say. It.* "I wished... she were dead."

Will reaches for my hand and touches it gently. "Oh, Ellie."

I swallow, overwhelmed. "I ran out of the house and slept at Jose's. The next morning when I came in, the house didn't feel right. There was a thickness in the air and an eerie silence. I walked down the hallway and opened the bathroom door. My mom was lying on the floor. Not breathing."

Will wraps his hand around mine. "I'm sorry you've

held all that inside. That wasn't your fault, Ellie. You can't blame yourself."

I shake my head. "Yes, I can. She was fragile. What I said tipped her over the edge."

"But, Eleanor, she made the choice. She made the decision – not you."

I start trembling, and tears rain down my cheeks. "Oh, Will...if only I could tell her how sorry I am, I would. I didn't mean it. I was so angry with her. Oh God, I killed her. I'm so sorry. Oh God, I'm sorry. So, so sorry."

Will doesn't say anything, but in the dark of the lighthouse, with the wind and the rain howling at me, Will reaches over and wraps me in his arms. I'm shaking uncontrollably. My stomach aches with regret, and my head hurts from all the pressure, but I said it. I told someone.

"Just cry, Eleanor. Let it out."

Will sits back against the wall and enfolds me in his arms. He holds me tight and kisses my head. "She knows you're sorry. That wasn't your fault, Ellie. It wasn't your fault."

I wail. I rock back and forth. All the sadness buried deep inside spills from the darkest place inside me.

Will knows my secret. It's isn't hidden anymore.

Spent and exhausted, I fall asleep in his arms.

good-bye to Henry

I wake with blankets wrapped around me. Will's nestled next to me, one arm tucked over me.

The storm is over. Sunrise is filtering into the cottage. My eyes are puffy from crying, and the light streaming through the windows hurts them. I squint, trying to adjust to the brightness.

Will rubs his eyes with one hand and snuggles in closer with the other. "Hey, there," he says. His voice is hoarse and quiet, and my stomach does a flip-flop.

"Hmm...morning," I say, quiet, pensive. I stretch and arch my back, shifting around. Then I lie still, thinking of everything he did for me.

"How do you feel this morning?" His voice is soft, careful, like he's picking his way through wreckage.

There's a calm inside me that hasn't been there in months, maybe ever. I'm not shaking anymore. "I'm better." I still have the deep guilt that's always a part of me, but relief's intermingled with it now.

Will reaches for my hand and interlaces our fingers.

"Can I tell you something?"

"Yes."

He hesitates, staring at the blanket we're both wrapped in. He plays with the edge of it. Then he takes a deep breath and looks at me, full in the face. His clear blue eyes are warm and affectionate. "I'm in love with you, Eleanor Martinson. Utterly and absolutely."

Those words, full of tenderness and risk, melt me. Anything still holding back inside, anything still protecting me from being hurt disappears. "I love you too, Will Larson."

He moves toward me and touches my face, drawing me toward him. I take a deep breath. His lips touch mine, and they're soft and taste of the morning.

He lifts his other hand to my cheek, and the kiss deepens. I put my arm behind his neck and run my hands through his silky hair. The world and all its problems disappear.

He finally pulls back, taking a deep breath. His eyes are intense. Safe intense. We stare at each other. He trails a finger down my face.

I finally break the silence. "So, you aren't going to kick me out of your room the next time I try and talk to you about your dad?"

Will's eyes change. "No, I won't. I've thought a lot about what you said. I need to figure it out with him. I don't know what's going to happen, but I can't keep punishing him anymore." He combs his fingers through my hair. "It's hurting me more than him." He touches his forehead against mine and lifts a few of my curls. "I'm so glad your hair is back to normal."

"You didn't like it straight?" I ask, surprised and grateful.

He shakes his head. "No, I couldn't stand your hair all straight."

I look at him to see if he's telling the truth.

He must think I'm offended because he pulls me close

and says, "You always look pretty. It was just that straight hair didn't seem like you. I like your wild hair." He lifts my chin and inhales for a few seconds, as if he's breathing me in.

"What's going to happen with us?" I ask.

He laughs. "We're going to hold hands, kiss, and talk all the time."

"More than friends?" He said he loved me last night, so I'm guessing yes.

He cups my cheek with his hand. "Considering that we both confessed we're in love with each other, I think we're more than friends." He kisses me again. "Thank you, Ellie," he whispers into my ear. "You changed my life."

I relax. He really does love me. It won't be perfect, and we'll probably fight a lot, but we're in it together. I stay quiet and stare at him for a minute. He's in love with me. *He's in love with me.* All of a sudden I'm lighthearted. "Do you want one of my puppies?"

"Maybe I'll give one to my dad," he says. "Like a peace offering."

"That sounds like a good idea," I say. "I'm going to give one to Prissy and the twins."

"And the other one?"

"I don't know, maybe we should give it to Alex."

Will scrunches up his face. "I still can't believe you kissed him."

I elbow him. "He kissed me. And how do you think I felt? Everyone kept telling me you were getting back together with Nadine."

"No." He looks confused. "I don't know who told you we were together, but we never were. I've been holding out for you the whole time."

I don't tell him it was Amy.

After a few minutes, when the puppies start to whimper, Will goes over and checks on them, and I start gathering up the blankets.

I stand and glance out the window, and Henry comes

to mind, I remember how transparent he seemed the last time I saw him. I want to make things right before he dies.

Will glances over. He's kneeling over the pups, petting the little black girl. "We need to get these puppies some water, Ellie."

"Sure. But I'd like to see if I could say something to Henry before we go."

Will nods and opens the front door, and sunlight streams inside. The birds chirp in the trees. The air smells fresh, like everything's been washed and cleaned. The clouds are disappearing. Remnants of the storm are scattered outside the lighthouse. Logs are floating and washing up onto the shore. Debris is strewn about everywhere. For the first time in a long, long while, my insides feel calm, like the storm inside of me has also quieted down.

I step outside and see Maggie lying dead on the ground in front of me. I stagger backwards. Sadness overwhelms me.

So many regrets. But there's one I can do something about.

"Henry," I yell. "Are you there?" I wait for a few moments, glancing about.

He comes stumbling through the woods. I can almost see through him, and Will, who is behind me, gasps. He winds his arm around my waist and holds me tight.

Henry stays a few feet away. But he sees Maggie there. "She's dead," he says.

I can't tell if he means Maggie or my mom.

"Yes, she is."

"Why did you call me?"

I fumble for words. Will steps even closer.

"I wanted to thank you for telling me the truth about my mom and the man from Chile."

Henry's eyes are sad. He totters around, glances at the sea. "I never told her how sorry I am."

"I know. I never got to tell her how sorry I am for what

I said to her either." I clear my throat. "Henry, I'm Rose's daughter, Eleanor."

He turns and smiles a bit, and I can see he believes me. "You really are Rose's daughter, aren't you?"

"I am."

"That's why you can see me."

"Maybe." But that doesn't explain why Will can see him. I step toward him. "I want to tell you something else. I think she'd want me to." I pause, swallow, and breathe in. "I want to say, um, that I forgive you." I didn't know if I could say it, but I did, and as the words come out, it's like an invisible weight falling off me. By extending forgiveness to him, perhaps someone will extend forgiveness to me.

He doesn't move. We stare at each other, and I exhale slowly. He gives me a curt nod. "Good-bye, Ellie."

"Good-bye, Henry."

He turns, but instead of walking back into the woods, he heads toward the cliff. He gives me one last glance, steps off, and vanishes.

Will and I watch the cliff for a moment, speechless. I shiver and tip my head to see Will. He's no longer staring at the cliff, but at me. His eyes are kind and honest and good, and I know what he feels for me goes deeper than he can explain.

The gaping hole that I've felt all summer feels like it's being sewn up now, put back together. His love is filling me up inside. It isn't spilling onto the ground anymore.

"I'm starving," I tell him. "You want breakfast?"

"Absolutely," he says. "What about Maggie?"

"Let's cover her with a blanket and come back after we eat.

"I'll do it." Will goes inside to get the wool blanket we folded by the door. He also picks up the pups and hands one to me. The puppies wiggle and whimper but calm down after a few moments.

We walk down the path leading to my house, in a silence that needs no words. When we get there, we wander around the back to find an empty apple box. We set it next to kitchen door and place the pups inside.

Violet is hanging up the phone with a perplexed expression on her face. She turns to me and rubs her forehead. "That was the hospital, Ellie."

I stand still. "What'd they say?"

"The nurse wanted me to tell you Henry passed away a few minutes ago. She said his face seemed almost peaceful."

I say nothing, but I'm grateful that I could give Henry what he needed to let go.

Violet glances at Will, and then over at me. "Why don't you two sit down? You look like you have a story to tell."

"First we have to take care of the puppies we found."

Violet follows us out to the porch. She leans over the apple box and peers inside. "Well, goodness gracious." She wipes her hands on her apron and helps me give them some water.

We get them settled and then sit down to tell Aunt Violet everything.

end of September

Later, after everything's calmer, I tell Violet I won't be going back to the trailer park. She and Ben and the kids are my family now, and I want to be with them. Violet cries and hugs me, and I hug her back.

Violet, Will, and I decide to have a celebration at the lighthouse and invite everyone to see what we did, and to celebrate my mother's life. Will thinks it would be cool for me to say a few words and do a memorial for her.

My aunt and uncle bake treats with the kids – chocolate chip cookies, apple pies, and brownies – to share with everyone. Amy, Mr. Larson, and Christine arrive on the ferry early in the morning. Jake and Alex walk over. Even Nadine makes it to the lighthouse. Best of all, Guadalupe, Maria, and Jose drive over to support me.

Everyone loves the lighthouse. I walk them through the cottage, pointing to all the things Will and I did. And then right before we begin the ceremony, Will stands off to the side with his dad for a moment and hands him the puppy we named Lightning. Mr. Larson laughs. He and Will shake hands, and afterwards his dad wipes his eyes.

We sit outside the lighthouse, in the open air, facing the sea. The sky is clear blue, the air is cooling down from the warm summer, and there's a hint of autumn in the air. The leaves are darkening to rich golds and browns.

Violet stands and tells some of the history of the lighthouse, shares a story about my mom when she was little, then says something I'll never forget. "I will always miss Rose." She catches my eye. "She was my younger sister and not a day goes by that I don't remember her beautiful smile. Rose could never be forgotten, and her legacy will continue on long after today in her beautiful daughter, Eleanor." She chokes up, and her hand shakes slightly. She looks over at me. "We are forever thankful that you came into our lives, Ellie."

When Violet's finished, she invites me to come up and share a few words. This is the speech I give:

"This lighthouse was my mother's favorite place during some of her happiest years. I miss her and will always wish she'd lived long enough to see so much more of life. In these months since she died, I've wandered around wondering what to do about my sadness and how to move on. I realize I may never move on completely. Part of me will always miss my mom and wish she'd lived longer. I doubt a day will go by when I won't feel regret over what happened to her, over things I said, or what I should or shouldn't have done. But, my mom wanted me to live. She wanted me to enjoy my life. And she wanted me to be strong, and I want to become strong for her.

"We invited you here today to celebrate and remember the life of Rose Martinson, my mother, a beloved sister, and a good friend. Mom, I miss you. May you rest in peace."

Everyone cries. Violet weeps, and Ben is blinking hard, but his face is beaming like he's proud of me. Even Will's eyes are brimming with tears. It seems like everyone's eyes are moist. Everyone, that is, except me. I finally feel like I've cried enough.

After everyone leaves, Will and I walk down to the beach. We sit on a log, and he asks why I didn't mention Henry.

"I thought about it, but I wasn't sure what to say. Besides, the celebration was supposed to be about my mom."

Will nods and gently puts his arm around me. I snuggle closer, rest my head against his shoulder, and breathe a sigh of relief. The relief someone might feel when they've returned home after a long and difficult journey.

"What's next?" he says and looks into my eyes. "Are we going to find your dad?"

"I think so, but not today. Today, I want to sit with you and watch the water go by.

about the author

Tina Bustamante grew up in the Seattle area. After high school she spent three years sailing around the world on a book ship that sold literature to developing countries. Tina studied at Northwest University and currently lives in Temuco, Chile, with her husband and her two children, along with their dog and pony. They are developing twenty-seven acres where they hope to live off the land.

If you enjoyed *As Waters Gone By*, you might enjoy these Leap Books...

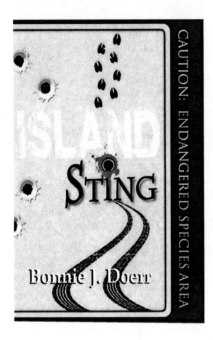

Island Sting

by Bonnie J. Doerr

Intrepid teens track down the poacher of the endangered Key deer. But will they survive when the killer turns from stalking deer to hunting humans?

Stakeout

by Bonnie J. Doerr

Involved in a new undercover sting, the Keys teens plan to save a different endangered species. This time they try to capture the criminals who are robbing sea turtle nests. Danger, intrigue, and mystery await them at every turn.

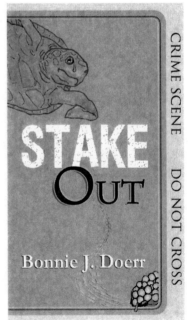

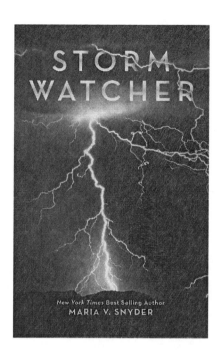

Storm
Watcher
by
Maria V. Snyder

The youngest son in a family of search-and-rescue dog trainers, Luke must face his deathly fear of storms to prove that her and the dog he's training belong in the family business.

Chase
by
Sydney Scrogham

In an epic battle of good and evil, Chase must gather his forces to defeat the cruel Snyx before it wipes out the land of miniature winged horses and destroys a human Chase loves.

Thank you for purchasing this Leap Books publication. For other exciting teen novels, please visit our online bookstore at www.leapbks.net.

For questions or more information contact us at leapbks@gmail.com

Leap Books
www.leapbks.net

CPSIA information can be obtained at www.ICGtesting.com
Printed in the USA
BVOW07s1310221013

334324BV00001B/1/P